EJECTED

The Story that Solves
the Climate Crisis

DAWN PAPE

GOOD GREEN LIFE
—publishing—

Good Green Life Publishing
P.O. Box 74 Circle Pines, MN 55414
www.goodgreenlifepublishing.com

The publisher is not responsible for websites
(or their content) referenced in this book.
First edition: October 2020

Library of Congress Cataloging-in-Publication Data

Names: Pape, Dawn, author
Title: Ejected—The Story that Solves the Climate Crisis | Dawn Pape
Description: First edition. | St. Paul: Good Green Life Publishing, 2020. | Includes bibliographical references. | Informational fiction.
Summary: This book tackles climate change by weaving stories with real solutions to combat the climate crisis. People with enormous carbon footprints are ejected from the planet. In order to return to Earth, "the Ejected" need to come together to figure out how to reverse the climate crisis. Solving the climate crisis is feasible as far as technology and economics are concerned. All that is missing to implement climate solutions is progressive leadership and the collective will to do so.
Identifiers: Library of Congress Control Number (LCCN): 2020940615 | ISBN 978-0-9971131-9-8 (paperback) | ISBN 978-1-7352427-0-5 (ebook)

[1. climate crisis education 2. climate solutions 3. environmental justice 4. empowerment 5. environmental education]

This book is dedicated to...
all of the idealists out there who prefer trying to make the
world a better place—and risk failing—over not trying at all.

And also to my late host-father, Dr. Horst-Jürgen Wienen,
who first brought our world's energy and climate problems
to my attention in 1987. Your wisdom and kindness are
dearly missed.

Contents

MISSION POSSIBLES

Preface

Solving the climate crisis is feasible, as far as technology and economics are concerned. All that is missing to implement climate solutions is progressive leadership and the collective will to do so. Although this story is fictional, it was built around real solutions to combat the climate crisis. The framework of the missions the characters embark on is based on solid scientific information, primarily from *En-ROADS* (Energy Rapid Overview and Decision-Support) policy simulator, Project Drawdown, and many other reputable information sources.

The En-ROADS Climate Change Solutions Simulator uses the best available science and has been extensively calibrated. The simulation model was developed by Massachusetts Institute of Technology (MIT) Sloan School of Management, Climate Interactive (a nonprofit think tank), and Ventana Systems (a company specializing in complex modeling). Project Drawdown is a nonprofit organization that aims to help the world reach "drawdown"— the future point in time when levels of atmospheric greenhouse gases begin to decline. This organization emerged as a leading resource for information and insight about climate solutions after its book *Drawdown* achieved New York Times best-seller status in 2017.

The graphs on the following three pages are from Climate Interactive (EnROADS Climate Change Solutions Simulator) showing an overview of what the average global temperature is predicted to be under three different senarios:

1. continue with the status quo resulting in an unlivable planet for humans within 80 years
2. implement a wide range of existing solutions explored in this book and barely maintain a livable planet for people
3. implement current technologies plus new technologies to remove carbon and to further limit temperature change

I hope this book will bring these critical solutions into daily conversation while providing a sense of urgency, empowerment and humor that will aid in uniting people to take global action. Without our solidarity, our trajectory is headed straight toward a climate unfit for humans within the foreseeable future. Why is there any hesitation in getting started?

Thank you, in advance, for reading. I look forward to coming together around issues that unite humanity and create a more just, loving, and sustainable world with you.

With love, peace, hope, and solidarity,

Dawn Pape
St. Paul, Minnesota
September 2020

climateinteractive.org/tools/en-roads/

Status Quo: Planet will warm ~7.3 ºF by 2100

If we continue with the status quo, our average global climate is predicted to warm ~7.3 ºF by 2100. This would be an unlivable climate for humans. Although 7.3 ºF isn't a big change on a daily basis, it is huge on a planetary scale. The last ice age was only 5-9 ºF cooler than the present global climate.

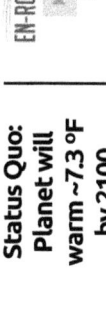

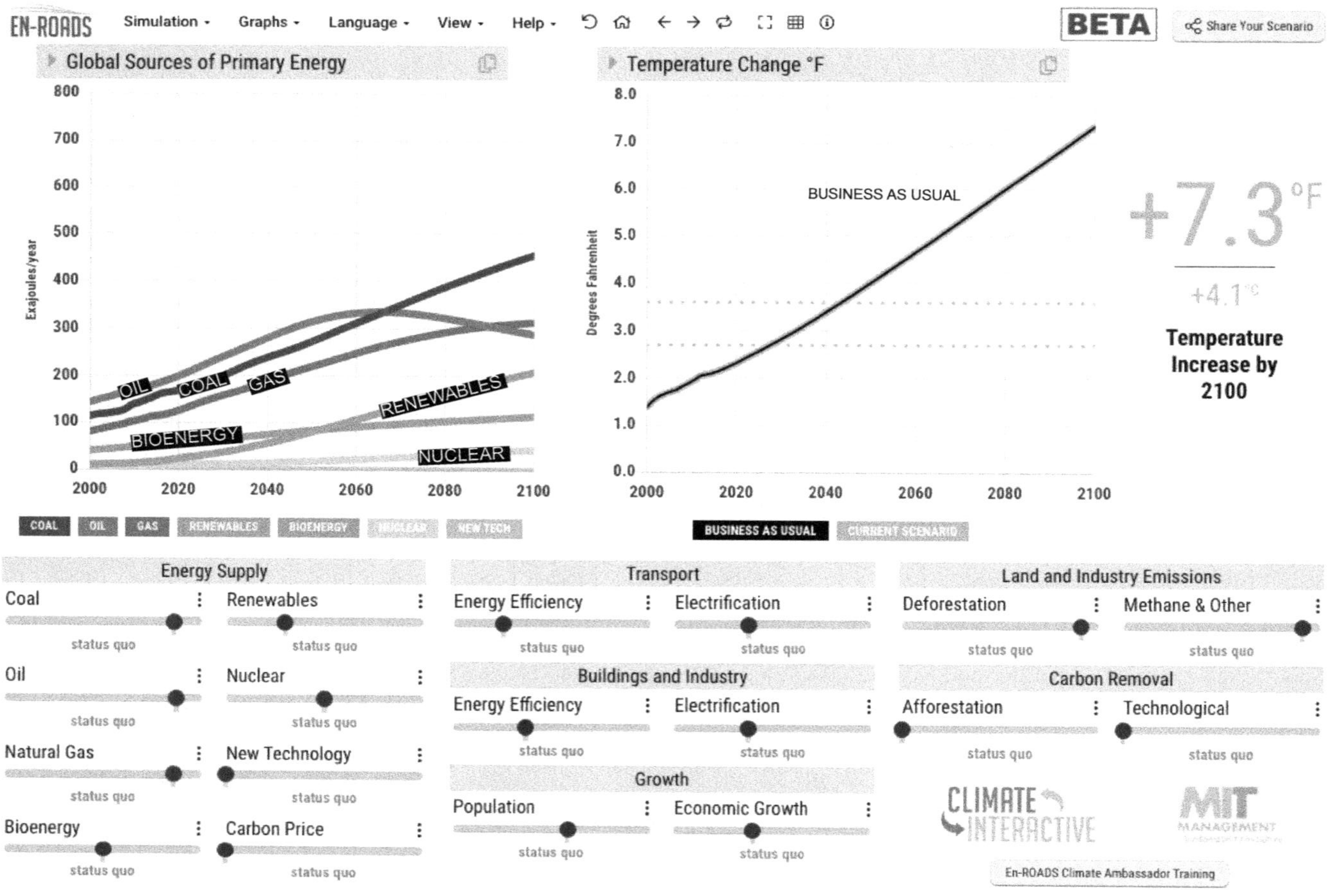

climateinteractive.org/tools/en-roads/

Implementing Today's Technologies: Planet will warm 3.1 °F by 2100

If we work as a global community to implement the types of changes discussed in *Ejected*, we can limit the average global climate change to ~3.1 °F. This is still above the target of 2.7 °F, but still likely a livable climate.

x

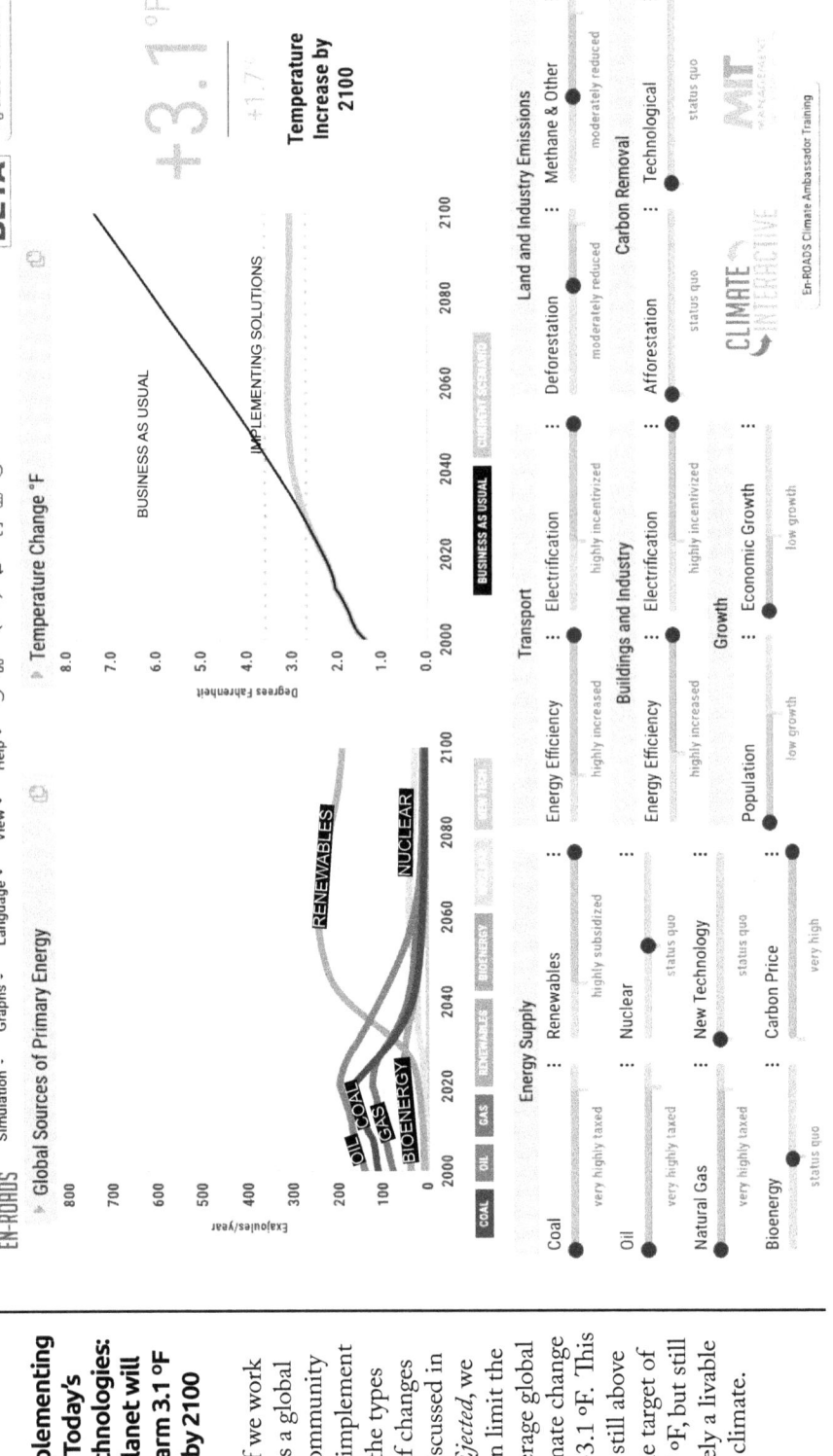

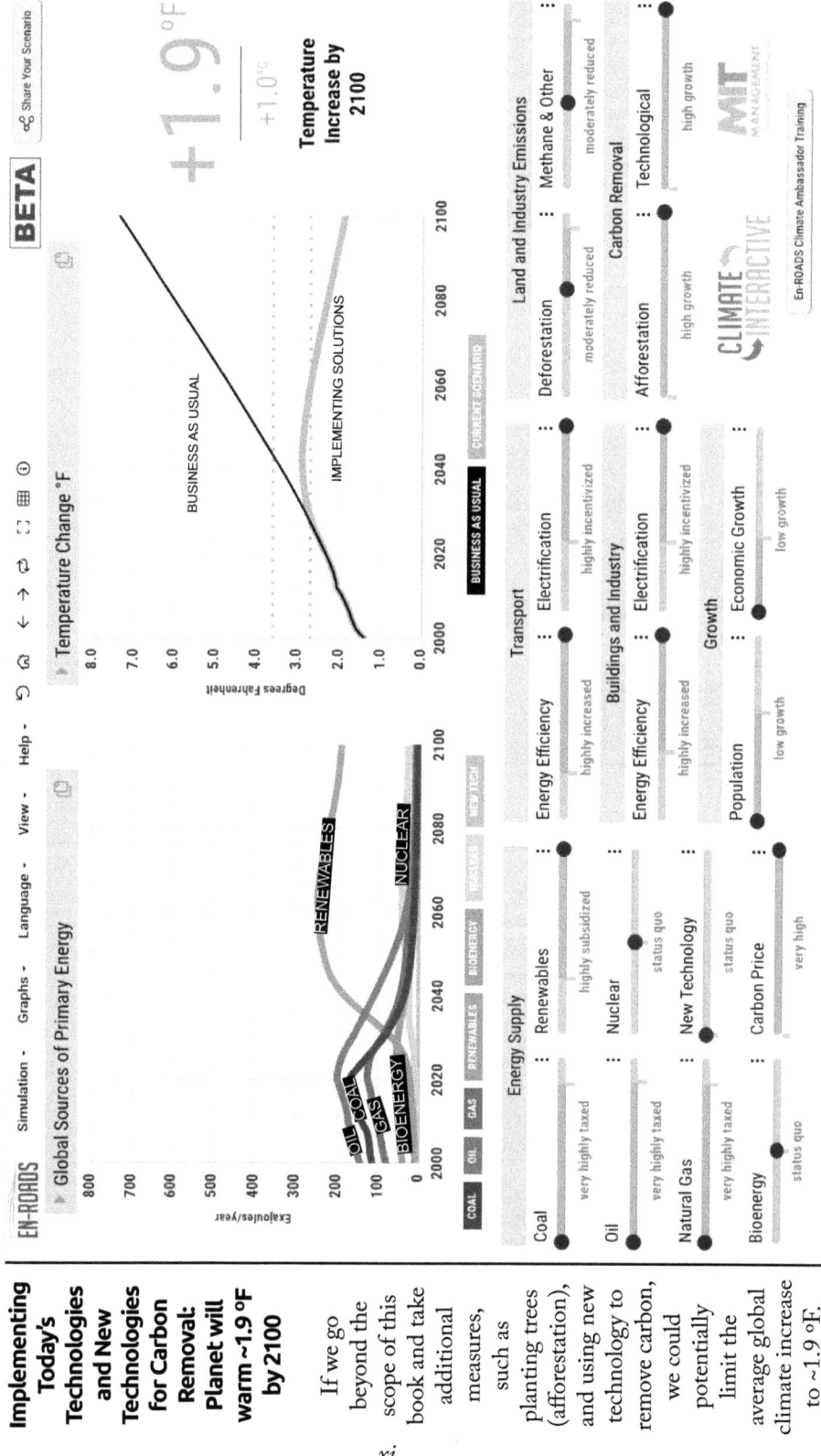

Implementing Today's Technologies and New Technologies for Carbon Removal: Planet will warm ~1.9 °F by 2100

If we go beyond the scope of this book and take additional measures, such as planting trees (afforestation), and using new technology to remove carbon, we could potentially limit the average global climate increase to ~1.9 °F.

Project Drawdown's
Table of Solutions

as of August 12, 2020

This table shows the impact of the characters' actions if they were implemented on a global scale according to information from *Project Drawdown. (https://www.drawdown.org/solutions/table-of-solutions)*

- Drawdown (CO_2e emissions) in Scenario 1 is roughly in-line with a 3.7 °F (2 °C) temperature rise by 2100.
- Drawdown (CO_2e emissions) in Scenario 2 is roughly in-line with a 2.7 °F (1.5 °C) temperature rise by 2100.

Chapter Number Title Character(s)	Practice(s)	Gigatons of CO_2e reduced worldwide from 2020-2050	
		Scenario 1 (+3.7 °F by 2100)	Scenario 2 (+2.7 °F by 2100)
11 Voilà Viola	Solar (concentrated, distributed, utility-scale)	88.9	211.73
	Wind (micro, onshore, offshore)	57.74	159.27
	Geothermal	6.19	9.85
	Hydropower	1.69	3.28
	Ocean power	1.38	1.38
	Building (smart thermostats, automation systems, insulation, high-performance glass, district heating, building retrofitting, net-zero buildings)	47.64	60.94
	total	203.54	446.45
13 The Cost of Hot Water Heather	Low-Flow Fixtures	0.91	1.56
	Solar Hot Water	3.59	14.29
	total	4.5	15.85

Chapter Number Title Character(s)	Practice(s)	Gigatons of CO_2e reduced worldwide from 2020-2050	
15 Flipping Farming **Doris**	Regenerative Agriculture Conservation Agriculture Nutrient Management Biochar production	14.52 13.40 2.34 2.22	22.27 9.43 12.06 4.39
	total	**32.48**	**48.15**
16 "Eating" Fewer Emissions **Nina, Ayesha, Nevaeh, Rachel, Pooja**	Reduce Food Waste Bioplastics Clean Cookstoves Biogass for Cooking	87.45 0.96 31.34 4.65	94.56 3.80 72.65 9.70
	total	**93.06**	**108.06**
17 Equitable Transporation **Bob**	Walkable Cities Bicycle Infrastructure Electric Bicycles Carpooling Public Transit High-Speed Rail Telepresence Hybrid Cars Efficient Trucks Electric Trains Electric Cars	1.44 2.56 1.31 7.70 7.51 1.30 1.05 7.89 4.61 0.10 11.87	5.45 6.65 4.07 4.17 23.36 3.77 3.80 4.63 9.71 0.65 15.68
	total	**47.34**	**81.94**
18 Ubuntu **Ricky**	Refrigeration Management Alternative Refrigerants	57.75 43.53	57.75 50.53
	total	**101.28**	**108.28**
19 Lifting Up All Women **Mohammed, Phil, Wei, Fang**	Education & Rights for Females	85.42	85.42
	total	**85.42**	**85.42**
	GRAND TOTAL	**567.62**	**894.15**

CHAPTER 1

The No-Show

Where is he? He's never late. Ivy wondered. But instead of being upset that her dad hadn't come yet to pick her up for the weekend, she decided to take the opportunity to relax. It had been a busy week, with soccer practice every night, before-school chamber orchestra practices, a piano lesson, mountains of homework, and the spring art show the previous night.

Even though she loved hanging out with her dad, she wasn't really looking forward to the coming weekend. She missed how things used to be with her dad before the divorce, back when it was the two of them hanging out. They'd always gone on lots of adventures together and would laugh the whole time. Her dad could make absolutely anything fun. One of her favorite things to do with her dad was to people-watch in public places. They would make up scenarios and narrate what strangers were thinking or saying. But now, there was always a girlfriend tagging along—and it usually wasn't the same one. Ivy didn't feel like she could be herself around any of these women, and she didn't know why they always had to come along. Ivy thought it was obvious that none of those women were even remotely compatible with her dad. She didn't know why her dad couldn't see it. She was convinced that her mom and dad still belonged together; they'd just lost their connection. Everyone else told her that she was just having trouble accepting the reality of the divorce, that she was in denial.

And lately, thought Ivy, *there was the endless nit-picking. When did Dad become such a nitpicker?* He would drill her on everything from mundane things like, "Did you brush your teeth?" and "Did you pack your snack?" or "How much water did you drink today?" to "Have you researched any colleges and scholarship opportunities?" *I'm fourteen, Dad. Take it easy.*

She found herself remembering the time he'd called from Colorado, during a skiing trip with his friends. *His first question was about how much fiber I'd had that day,* thought Ivy. *Who asks that? Not to mention who asks their 14-year-old daughter that? I mean, how socially awkward. Like right away, too, before you talk about normal stuff like what you did that day, or what made you laugh recently? You didn't ask me what I'd been reading, or what I found interesting? How I'd helped to make the world a better place today? If there is anything on my mind? Nope, none of that. It's just so weird, Dad.* She knew that her dad's urge to control every detail was just his anxiety popping up, but it wasn't fun to be around him when he was like that. Her dad just didn't seem to be happy and it seemed he felt the need to make others feel his unhappiness too, through his constant badgering and complaining that things weren't quite meeting his unrealistic expectations.

He's never late, so he must have a pretty decent excuse, she decided. She didn't even feel like doing Instagram, so just closed her eyes and melted into her mom's awesome couch.

CHAPTER 2

Ejected

Stuck in traffic, Keith could feel his blood pressure rising. He was late for picking up his daughter, Ivy, and he was *never* late. It was a perfect evening to stroll around Grand Avenue and he was excited to see her and take her out for pizza and ice cream. He'd had to travel for work last weekend, so he hadn't seen her for nearly two weeks. It felt like an eternity to Keith. He missed her.

He also detested situations he couldn't control—like being stuck in traffic. *Deep breaths*, he reminded himself, *I don't have to let this get to me. I am in control of how I react to stressful situations*, he repeated this mantra to himself, just like his meditation app told him, over and over.

But the freeway was like a parking lot, and he had not moved in several minutes. He had the top down on his convertible and, without air movement, it was getting hot and uncomfortable. He loosened his tie as he impatiently rechecked his phone, but it still showed traffic as red in all directions. He was annoyed that the navigation lady had not warned him of this slowdown and that there was no escape route.

Keith closed his eyes, leaned his head against the steering wheel and consciously took a deep belly breath, then exhaled to the count of four. He knew he had to do better at managing his stress; he could definitely feel something was wrong with his heart, and it scared him.

Again, he inhaled slowly and deeply. But as he started to exhale, his eyes involuntarily flew open and sheer terror caused him to hold his breath. He had the sensation that he was shooting up into space like a missile. He felt just like he was on the *Disney World Epcot* theme park Mission: SPACE simulator ride that his daughter loved so much. He had hated that ride then and had resolved to never subject himself to the torture again. Moments later, the sickening g-force feeling subsided and was replaced with overwhelming nausea and dizziness. He exhaled and focused on trying not to throw up.

He looked around, but there were no longer tail lights or a steering wheel in front of him. He couldn't see a thing. It was utterly dark, and he wasn't in his car anymore. He was standing in nothingness surrounded by darkness.

He panicked and wondered, *Have I gone blind? Did I have a stroke or a heart attack?* He started reciting the alphabet in an attempt to ground himself. He could recite it easily, without slurred speech, so he decided it couldn't have been a stroke. He continued to search his mind for answers. *Have I died? Am I dreaming? Did I lose consciousness?* He scanned the darkness and prayed to see even a small flicker of light or a dim shadow.

He turned in circles but saw only blackness. *Where am I?* He waved his arms back and forth like he was an air traffic controller on a landing strip signaling a plane to land. Nothing. He felt nothing. The air around him wasn't hot or cold, humid or dry. It was simply black and still. He dropped to his knees and started to crawl, but he couldn't tell what he was crawling on. There seemed to be no floor beneath him. He kept creeping on all fours, hoping he would feel something, anything that would bring him to somewhere he recognized. He longed for something that made sense. He longed to see his daughter. He just wanted to know whether he was alive or not.

On he inched, feeling his way through the darkness. He was scared, and he pledged to himself that he'd live a better life if he ever got out of this place or if this bizarre nightmare ever ended. He silently repeated, *Please, please, please, please, pleeeease*, over and over as he crawled through the empty and dark abyss. He didn't have a good sense of time, but he feared it would never end. *Maybe this is purgatory?* he wondered.

Just when he'd convinced himself that his situation would never change, it did. The blackness began to fade, and he saw a mesmerizing, bluish glow with swirls of white beneath him. *The Earth! I can see the Earth? If planet Earth is below me, where in the world am I?* he wondered. *Or, rather where in the universe am I?* he corrected himself since he clearly wasn't "in the world."

In the distance, he saw an enormous crowd of people standing and casually conversing with each other in dim light. The scene reminded him of observing a crowd during a theater intermission. But this group was the most beautiful, diverse assembly of people he'd ever seen. They represented every skin tone, gender, and body type and wore brightly colored clothes. He was drawn to them and the sound of their musical chatter. He felt relief simply knowing that wherever he was, he wasn't alone. But then he thought, *Now I know I must be dreaming.*

Shaking his head and opening his eyes wide to wake himself, he slapped his cheek. The others were now watching him crawl towards them and laughing. They weren't really laughing at him, but because they knew what he was going through. One by one, people had been taken to this strange place in the same way, and nearly everyone had the same reaction—attempting to slap themselves awake like he was doing. He stood up, feeling a little silly and self-conscious for still being on his hands and knees. Keith marveled at the faces he saw and kept turning in circles, trying to make sense of what he was seeing.

It seemed as though Keith was the final arrival because a group of teenagers, or young adults—Keith couldn't exactly tell their age—started calling everyone's attention. Although diverse in appearance, this group of youth shared a remarkably similar air of confidence.

"Listen up, Boomers and Deniers!" called out a muscly teenager who reminded Keith of a human version of a Rottweiler.

"And don't forget Unaware and Apathetic!" called another young man.

Nodding, the first guy hollered, "I know you all want to know why you're here. If I can get your attention, I'll explain." About half of the people in the noisy crowd obeyed the suggestion to quiet down until the teen roared, "Hey! I said, LISTEN UP!" With that order, the crowd hushed instantly.

"You people need some sense knocked into you. We've been hammering on you for decades, hoping it wouldn't come to this, but you just had to keep ignoring us. And now, now it has come to this," barked the Rottweiler-guy. "There is a climate crisis that needs to be solved. Everyone needs to put their differences aside and solve it. It's like COVID-19 on steroids."

Insulted, a lady in pearls huffed. "Some sense? I have a Ph.D. I have plenty of 'sense' and several degrees to prove it," she retorted.

"Shut it, Martha!" boomed the adolescent with a deep voice that could've belonged to a grown man. In an instant, his nose was an inch from hers, and this woman, who was apparently named Martha, did, indeed, stop talking.

Keith stood with his arms crossed over his chest. He wasn't impressed by these demanding adolescents who were calling them names. He looked around to see the other victims' faces. Their expressions ranged from confusion and boredom to fear and disdain.

The Rottweiler-like one continued, "You all have been ejected from Earth because it cannot sustain your selfish, massive impacts. Your greenhouse gas emission footprints are despicable, and most of you have been actively denying climate change. 'Climate has changed before,' you argue, or, 'It's the sun.' Some people say, 'It's not a bad thing.' How dumb are you? Of course, it's a bad thing! Will you finally think it's a bad thing when the climate changes so quickly that your food supply cannot adapt and you are short on food? Or how about when the weather is so unstable that it is just a matter of time until there is another supercell hurricane or tornado?"

Another young leader, who had enormous teeth that reminded Keith of a horse, chimed in, "And here's a doozy, how about when people say 'there is no consensus'?"

At this, the dog guy dropped to his knees, laughing. That statement evidently cracked him up, because he could hardly get his response out. He sputtered, "Or... how... about... 'models are unreliable'?"

Without missing a beat in the verbal volley, the guy Keith decided to call Seabiscuit, panted, "And Antarctica is actually gaining ice!"

Dog guy and Seabiscuit were now doubled over laughing while the crowd looked around uneasily.

In the next blink, however, both of the young men were standing tall and rigidly shouting in unison with their arms stretched out in front of them like they were choking the air, "To all of this denial we say SHAME! ON! YOOOOU!"

With each of those three words, the Ejected experienced increasing and unbearable physical pain. Some people cried out and clutched their chests, while others gasped for air and shook as though they were being electrocuted. With pleading eyes, each of the Ejected prayed for this trauma to end as they stared at the angry young men, who now had veins popping out all over their bodies. "Your actions have put the world in peril, and now it's up to you to fix your sins," the two young men said and, with that, they released their grip on the crowd, who let out a collective sigh.

"Now, let me just answer some FAQs," continued the dog man, as if nothing had happened. "Yes, you all are from different parts of the world. You all are hearing me in your native language. I am universal. When you talk to others, just speak as you normally would. You will be understood as if you are speaking the same language as the person you are talking to."

Fascinating, thought Keith. I wonder how I can tap into this technology and market it. Keith loved investing in new technologies.

But his thoughts were interrupted by the dog man, who was now demanding his attention. "Keith! Stay focused. Your greed is what got you here. You cannot market this language 'technology.' You are in another realm right now, remember?"

Well, I didn't actually know I was in a different realm until you just told me now, thought Keith. But he decided it would be better not to offer a retort.

At this point, a young woman with glasses stepped forward and glared at dog man. She spoke in an even tone, "While Seth is correct in what he said, I see from your body language that you aren't very open to it. No one likes to be shamed, accused, or called names," she said, as she turned her head with narrowing, laser-like eyes to the dog man, apparently named Seth, so he would take the hint to calm down.

"My name is Aziza," started the reasonable young lady. "Let me start from the beginning. We are the Defenders of the Future, and we have been living here, in the atmosphere, since 1975. The timing coincided with the publication of Columbia University professor and researcher Wallace Smith Broecker's article that correctly predicted that rising carbon dioxide—or CO_2—levels in the atmosphere would lead to unwanted 'global warming.'[1] It was clear that this scientist didn't have the pizazz to rock the world as much as the world needed to be rocked. So, we arrived here to help spread his message that climate change is real and caused by humans. We made the awful mistake of calling it 'global warming' at first, which opened the door to all kinds of skepticism. We now know it should've been called climate change from the beginning, because the changes it causes aren't consistent across the globe. But, overall, it's still true that the average global temperature is rising and the Earth as a whole is warming."

"Are you angels?" Interrupted a tiny gray-haired woman, as she pinched Seth's muscly arm.

"You could call us that," he replied, "but stop pinching me! Ow. Now!" The little lady sat down but continued her questioning, "Which god put you here?"

"Oh, here we go," he said, with a clenched jaw, clearly aggravated.

"Listen, I'm not going to get into a religious discussion right now. We don't have time for that. But as far as I can tell, you can call the force that unites us anything you want to: God, Allah, Brahman, spiritually enlightened one. The universal force behind every religion is true love that is free of selfishness and greed. And, seriously, it's time to stop fighting over how you pray, or if you pray, or meditate or whatever. Right now, we are facing whether or not our species will survive. Some people talk about 'saving the Earth,' but that's extraordinarily stupid. The Earth doesn't need saving. The Earth has been here for about 4.6 billion years and will continue to exist whether humans survive or not. The real question at hand is this: are humans smart enough to save themselves?"

Aziza nodded and acknowledged Seth as she took control of the conversation. "At this point, it's not looking good. We've been trying for forty-five years to get you people on board but, so far, we have failed miserably. We thought all we had to do was show you all the objective facts about the looming environmental problems—namely biodiversity loss and climate change caused by overconsumption of fossil fuels and overpopulation—and that you humans would respond accordingly. We thought that since people were capable of logic and reason, knowing the objective facts would be enough to make you all do the right things to protect the planet—and yourselves. But we were, oh, so very and utterly wrong. What we did not realize is that solid science and objective facts are no match for selfishness, greed, and apathy."

"How did you send us these so-called 'objective facts'?" asked Keith, gesturing air quotes with his fingers.

"By placing enlightened people all over the world," explained Aziza, wearily.

"I don't buy it," said Keith, regretting it as soon as the words left his lips, asking himself why he always needed to be such an extrovert and process his thoughts aloud.

"Buy it? BUY IT? There's nothing to 'buy' here, Keith," hollered Seth. "We are not selling you anything, Keith. We are explaining the situation of the world. We're not asking you. We are telling you that this is the way it is."

Keith fought the urge to reply and sat in silence.

"The climate crisis is a leadership crisis." Seth continued, "To transform society this decade, we need transformational leadership. And you sorry souls are our leaders, I guess. The only way for you to get back to Earth with your loved ones is for you to correct the environmental crimes against humanity that you have committed and to put the planet on a positive trajectory."

Aziza interjected to explain, "The fossil fuel industries were very effective in lobbying and casting doubt on whether the climate science was true. These greedy companies were just afraid of losing their profits, so they kept bringing up points that they knew would appeal to simple-minded, selfish, and apathetic citizens. And now, here we are today. We have about ten years to turn this situation around. All of you have either actively refuted that the climate crisis is happening or have been too apathetic to care. Some of you actively helped the bad guys, and some of you are the bad guys."

At this remark, the crowd of Ejected couldn't help looking around to try to figure out who the so called 'bad guys' were among them.

Aziza called the group's attention again and continued, "NASA nailed it when they reported that the Earth's average temperature has increased about two degrees Fahrenheit during the twentieth century."[2] Looking around at the group, she continued, "I see by the looks on your faces you're wondering what the big deal is? Two degrees may sound like a small amount because, on a daily basis, it is. But it's an unusual event in our planet's recent history. The Earth's climate record, which is preserved in tree rings, ice cores, and coral reefs, shows that the global average temperature should be far more stable than that and over much longer periods of time. Small changes in temperature correspond to enormous changes in the environment. For example, at the end of the last ice age, when the Northeast United States was covered by more than 3,000 feet of ice, average temperatures were only five to nine degrees Fahrenheit cooler than today."[3]

The Defenders of the Future lined up and looked at each of the Ejected squarely in the eyes as they jabbed each individual in the chest declaring their personal environmental sins for everyone to hear:

"You helped roll back mileage standards to boost big oil. And you always feel the need to be right."

"You mishandled refrigerant chemicals by dumping loads of refrigerators illegally."

"You denied countless women education."

"You used traditional agriculture instead of regenerative agriculture."

"You wouldn't build ultra-energy-efficient passive houses because it cost you more money upfront."

"You blocked ordinances that would have required net-zero houses to be built."

"You blocked clean energy sources."

"You went on a crusade against clotheslines, banning them across the U.S. because you just didn't like how they looked."

Keith tuned out and occupied himself by watching peoples' priceless expressions as they were publicly condemned. His thoughts were interrupted by Seth as he jabbed Keith's chest and bellowed, "And you. You lobbied against the carbon tax,"

"So, you think climate change is actually real," said a stupid man with the name Stanley embroidered on the top left side of his shirt. The entire assemblage of Ejecteds turned to look at him and hollered, "Yes!" in unison. Stanley looked offended that everyone had barked at him and put up his hands in his own defense.

The Defenders of the Future looked at each other and gave each other a subtle, nearly imperceptible nod. They knew that these deniers were well on their way to becoming believers. But they wanted to make sure the new believers understood the full impact of their actions, so they decided it was time to give the tours.

CHAPTER 3

The Tours

Without warning, and still recovering from their physical torment, the Ejected were catapulted in different directions. Keith watched with amusement as others' arms and legs flailed, and they all made the exact same ridiculous, wide-eyed, open-mouthed, terrified expression. He thought it was funny until he was catapulted, too. He found himself not only flailing, wide-eyed, and open-mouthed but screaming as well.

Some people were catapulted in groups, but Keith was alone with his Defender of the Future. The Defender was too angry to introduce himself or try to make small talk. Keith felt there was something familiar about his Defender but didn't know why.

What Keith didn't know was that his Defender had been observing him throughout his entire life. Because of this long history, the Defender knew Keith was capable of selflessness that served the greater good. But during the last decade, when given a choice, the Defender watched Keith make self-serving choices over and over. The Defender had lost patience with Keith. He'd decided it was time for a little tough love.

The Defender looked straight ahead, struggling to concisely explain decades of injustice. He feared being long winded would allow Keith to tune out. Finally, the Defender began to speak in a direct and even tone. He turned to Keith and stared him straight in the eyes so it was impossible for Keith to look away. "Twenty-five fossil fuel producers are responsible for half of the global emissions in the past three decades," the Defender explained, "and one hundred oil, coal, and gas companies are linked to seventy-one percent of emissions since 1988."[4]

"Half? Seventy-one percent?" echoed Keith. He knew fossil fuels were responsible for emissions, but he actually hadn't realized it was that much. Keith was learning not to argue with the Defenders, so he just looked down at his feet. He was having a hard time processing what this meant and the destruction that he was a part of.

"You lobbied for nearly all of these fossil fuel companies. It's your job to prevent further destruction now. Years ago, Georgina Gustin laid it all out in the Carbon Disclosure Project that traced the greenhouse gas emissions. More was emitted over the last three decades than during all of the previous two centuries. To be more specific, fossil fuel producers contributed 833 *gigatons* of CO_2 equivalent in the last twenty-eight years, compared with the 820 gigatons total that was produced during the previous 237 years."[5]

Wow. That's about ten times faster than the natural rate, thought Keith before sheepishly asking, "What did you mean by carbon dioxide equivalent?"

The guide answered, "There are many types of greenhouse gases. Carbon dioxide makes up the largest portion, and is the most talked about, but other gases—like methane, nitrous oxide, ozone, and chlorine and fluorine-containing solvents and refrigerants play a role, too. Gases like nitrous oxide are less common but about 300 times more damaging. In order to compare these gases, we need to compare apples to apples, so we use a math formula to do that to make them equal. So, if the greenhouse gas that we're talking about isn't actually carbon dioxide, but is lesser-talked-about methane or something, we say carbon equivalent."

Keith nodded, and the unnamed Defender stated flatly, "You knew lobbying for fossil fuels wasn't right, but you did it anyway. You justified your actions by saying, 'If I don't do this, someone else will.' Now you need to know the consequences of your actions."

Bewildered, Keith asked, "How do you know so much about me? What is your name?"

"My name is Salomon Asger Vester the third and I knew you before you were born. I knew your mother too," replied the Defender, hoping Keith would make the connection.

"Salomon Asger Vester?" Keith whispered, "From West Denmark?"

Salomon nodded.

"You're my grandpa?" said Keith slowly with disbelief.

Again, Salomon nodded.

"But you're young! Mom said you lived to be 81," exclaimed Keith.

"Age is irrelevant in the realm, son. I chose my favorite age when I arrived here," said his grandpa.

While Keith's head spun, his legs crumpled beneath him. The arguments he had been formulating about how developing countries were to blame evaporated. He was talking to his grandpa! Although he had never met this man before, his mom spoke of his honesty and character every day of her life. He was a legend and known for his kindness. Everyone in town who knew Keith's grandpa had heartwarming stories to share about his integrity, helpfulness, and humility.

As Keith stood before his grandpa, he felt ashamed that he had made a living as a lobbyist by mastering the blame game—pointing fingers, and making baseless accusations to purposefully muddy the waters and cast doubt on indisputable facts. Keith's voice was his power, but he found himself speechless.

Keith suddenly floated above a flooded village. Although he couldn't tell exactly what had happened, he could see that the people in the village were utterly destitute. Every house was submerged underwater, and the stench of sewage stuck to the back of his throat and made him gag. The town square was empty. People looked hungry, and their eyes were downcast. The only sounds were from children running and playing despite the filth and destruction that surrounded them.

Salomon explained, "What you're looking at here are the latest climate refugees. These 'natural' disasters are a result of our world's changing climate. With an overall warmer world, we have more evaporation, resulting in more moisture in the atmosphere. This excess moisture makes for a very turbulent atmosphere that is ripe for unstable weather patterns, like supercell hurricanes and tornadoes. The sea level is also rising as the ice caps are melting. The ocean salinity is changing, which is changing the fish populations, and people are losing the fish they depend on to eat. Simultaneously, their crops are being washed away.

"So, they have to move," Keith acknowledged. "You know that moving isn't the end of the world." Keith wanted to add "Grandpa" at the end of that statement but didn't. Even though this man was kin, he could tell Salomon meant to hold him at a distance.

"Sure, a move within your own country might not seem like a big deal, but consider the fact that skills such as herding, fishing, and farming are not going to be useful in urban areas. So, once these people move, work will be hard to find. These good people are also losing their social networks—their friends and family, their identities, and their culture," explained Salomon.

"OK," Keith conceded, "I see we have some refugees. But how many, really? How big of a problem could this possibly be?"

"Try about twenty-five million. And the number of climate refugees is expected to double over the next five years. It's predicted that as many as one billion people will be displaced by climate change over the next forty years. In fact, the United Nations estimates that more people are displaced due to climate change than war."[6]

"Wow. That's a lot. At least it's not killing people, though," said Keith attempting to make the situation not seem so dire.

"Ha! Climate change is absolutely already killing people!" hollered Salomon, "Air pollution alone kills *seven million* people each year.

That accounts for one in eight deaths.[7] And when you factor in secondary problems caused by climate change—like heat stress, malnutrition, malaria, diarrhea, vector-related illnesses, wildfires, hurricanes, and flooding—you could say there are lives being lost due to climate change. So just *stop* making excuses for your inaction."

Again, Keith wanted desperately to defend himself to alleviate his guilt. He also wanted to un-see those skinny, sickly bodies and all the poverty he'd witnessed. He closed his eyes to block the awful scene and kept them squeezed shut until Salomon told him sternly to open them. He reluctantly reopened his eyes to find that he was in a wetland, thick with mosquitoes. He swatted and ran in a pointless attempt to outrun the swarm.

"Increased rainfall and rising global temperatures are expanding the habitat and the breeding season of mosquitoes, exposing more people to diseases like dengue, chikungunya, Zika, Nipah, and Q fever," said Salomon unfazed by the swarming mosquitoes. "These conditions also breed vector-borne diseases caused by parasites, viruses, and bacteria transmitted by mosquitoes, ticks, flies, and fleas."

Keith jumped and wildly swung his arms in a futile attempt to escape the high-pitched buzz of the mosquitoes that voraciously bit him through his clothes.

"Climate change also opens the door to communicable diseases, Keith. As human-caused climate change has taken hold over the last several decades, dozens of new infectious diseases have emerged or begun to threaten new regions, including Zika and Ebola. Cholera is also becoming more difficult to control because the warm, brackish waters and rising sea levels help spread the disease. Cholera infects about four million people each year and kills about 100,000 of them."[8]

The Defender paused before continuing, "Ever heard of the bubonic plague?

"Of course, spread by rats and fleas during the Middle Ages. We kicked that disease eons ago though," Keith replied.

"Well, it wasn't actually eradicated; it was just controlled, so it became less common. And now it's increasing thanks to warmer springs and wetter summers, Keith."

Keith was again speechless, and the words *bubonic plague* tumbled around in his brain.

"Now let's talk about deadly bacteria called anthrax," said the Defender. "The anthrax spores are released from soil by thawing permafrost and seem to be spreading farther as a result of stronger winds."[9]

Keith thought about these huge numbers compared with the global response to the COVID-19 pandemic, which was caused by the novel coronavirus. *When the global death toll hit 20,000 people in the middle of March 2020,[10] global activity had come to a near screeching halt, as people around the globe quarantined. Climate change is already causing substantial death tolls, yet there is virtually no response.*

"That's right," the guide said, responding to Keith's thoughts. It freaked Keith out that his thoughts were no longer private.

Salomon explained, "People aren't acting collectively on climate change, although it's changing everything. It is the basis of most of the disturbances that have been hitting the news. People see the tragedies as unrelated and keep putting Band-Aids on the consequences. Climate change needs to be addressed from every angle. Just as people chipped in to do their part with stopping COVID-19, so must humanity come together to halt the climate crisis. And it's your job to stop the bleeding."

Keith was holding his breath, trying to find calmness in the swarm of mosquitoes. It seemed to work! He no longer heard the insanity-producing, shrill whine of the mosquitoes.

He opened his eyes to realize that he didn't hear the mosquitoes because he was no longer in the wetland. He saw the world off in the distance looking like a beautiful, blue marble just like he had when he'd first arrived with the Ejected. Judging from the size of the Earth, he decided he must be in the mesosphere. An overwhelming sense of peace relaxed his body. He felt serene and connected to the universe, with no pain or discomfort. Warmth and positivity surged through him. This was the best feeling he'd ever experienced. Euphoric. Clear-headed. Dark, but utterly peaceful, he acknowledged his state and wanted to exist in it forever.

Unfortunately, the feeling didn't last, and the smell of smoke overwhelmed him. He was on land again, but this time in a dry landscape. He turned in circles to find fires surrounding him in every direction. The heat was unbearable. He wanted to run, but there was no way out. As the fires came closer, the smell of burning flesh overtook him, and he threw up. The smoke choked him. He gasped as he prayed for air. The smoke stung his eyes, and he curled up in a little ball with his shirt and arms over his head. He knew he was powerless, and again he surrendered to the world.

With what he thought was his last breath, he was compelled to open his eyes. He was shocked to see that there were no longer fires surrounding him. Now his only thought was water. He needed water. His tongue was swollen. He looked down to see that his body looked like the skin and bones of a concentration camp prisoner. He held his bleeding nose as he staggered around in search of water.

"You are currently experiencing the effects of wildfires, dehydration, and famine caused by drought," said Salomon, obviously upset to see another being—especially his own grandson—in such a miserable state. But he had tried for decades to teach Keith from afar and point out the moral path, but Keith was stubborn and didn't seem to learn lessons. Salomon firmly believed there was a place for corporal punishment to make a lesson stick.

Keith couldn't verbally respond, so he slowly shook his head. As soon as Keith surrendered to the situation, he was ejected to hover above a mountain top. This time, Keith was too weak to even flail.

Keith looked down and saw glaciers! *Oh, blessed, beautiful sight!* The air was crisp and fresh. But terror replaced his elation as the glaciers avalanched down, crashing into the sea. Everywhere he looked, the glaciers slid away. He gasped and was catapulted to an Arctic region where he watched a bony polar bear swim to an ice floe and struggle to pull itself up on top of it. The starving bear looked around with no prospects of food in sight. He could feel that bear's exhaustion, and he had an incredible urge to lie down. He would do anything to sleep. To drink. To get the smell of burning flesh out of his nose, and to have his eyes stop stinging.

That, of course, didn't happen. Instead, he was ejected back into the mesosphere again, where he could see the lower 48 states before him like a map. A clock ticked under his view that showed the passage of years. The clock started in 2020 and went to 2100, then started over. He examined the regions one by one, starting from the top left as if he were reading a book.

In the Northwest region, he saw reduced water supplies, the sea level rise, and increased ocean acidification that limited fishing and aquaculture. There was not enough food, and he saw signs of massive malnutrition. Erosion, caused by the flooding, threatened the utility lines and he could see that power was unreliable as the light from cities flickered on and off. Wildfires that ravished the area were followed by insect outbreaks and tree diseases, causing widespread tree die-off.[11]

In the Midwest, where he lived when he wasn't lobbying in Washington, D.C., he witnessed extreme heat, followed by torrential downpours and flooding, which devastated agriculture and caused widespread hunger. The rich, precious topsoil created by the prairies that once covered the region, slipped away into rivers. The sediment found its way to the Gulf of Mexico, where it choked out the aquatic life there. The Great Lakes were largely evaporated and choked with invasive species. The flooding disrupted transportation and cell towers.[12]

Tears streamed down his face as he looked toward the Northeast, where he saw more heatwaves, followed by further heavy downpours and even higher sea levels. He witnessed towns slipping into the ocean; and infrastructure, agriculture, fisheries, and ecosystems collapse.[13]

Hoping for a positive scene, he looked toward the majestic Southwest, only to see the bleakness extend: intolerable heat, drought, dwindling water supplies, insect outbreaks, and wildfires.[14]

He couldn't stand another minute of this. He would do anything to make this all stop. *Just please make this all stop,* he thought over and over. *Please, please, please, please.*

Against his will, the tour continued, and he saw the Southeast's sea level rise so much that it destroyed the region's fishing economy and swallowed up homes and businesses at a breakneck pace. The extreme heat devastated the people's ability to work, and the lack of clean freshwater made survival in this region difficult.[15]

"Make it stop!" yelled Keith as he threw himself down on the ground and wept. "Just make it stop. I can't take this anymore! How can I make this stop?"

CHAPTER 4

The Reckoning

Although Keith was floating above the Earth, his soul was painfully heavy. His head throbbed, and his stomach churned. He was hopeless and miserable. Guilty. Lost. Banished.

He longed to be with his daughter, Ivy, who was, without question, the best part of his life. Ivy was smart, kind, honest, and hilarious. She'd told him that he was a good guy, but was working for the bad guys. How was she so insightful?

Until Ivy had started school, Keith was her primary caregiver while his wife, Viola, continued her career in renewable energy policy. *Those days with Ivy were the happiest days of my life,* remembered Keith. Ivy was always raring to go around 6:30 a.m. with a full agenda of things to do that day. She pretty much called the shots, but Keith was generally OK with her plans because she had such interesting ideas.

Together they'd collected fall leaves and learned the tree names, splashed in puddles, had picnics, gone on bike rides and hikes, and planted gardens. Every day was filled with joy, giggles, snuggles, and adventure. Being with Ivy made everything more fun. Perhaps it was how enthusiastic she was about everything and how she had entertaining commentary about everything. Keith's sister once joked that he could rent her out since she was so much fun. Keith and Ivy shared a solid bond.

Keith thought wistfully about how he had fallen in love with his ex-wife because she was so full of love, passion, and life—like Ivy. Viola was the ultimate do-gooder, who sought out problems to fix in her community and chipped in to help solve them, often anonymously. She was selfless, mindful, present, and put the common good before her own needs.

Keith and Viola met at a rally against fossil fuels in 1988—the year the world declared that climate change was caused by humans. He thought of the days they'd spent picnicking by prairies and watching the butterflies flutter by. They'd had a quiet life filled with farmers' markets, small gatherings with friends, home-brewed beer, and social and environmental causes that often involved music.

But when Ivy started school, Keith knew that they needed to make more money. Viola's altruistic career in renewable energy policy at a small non-profit was low paying. He took a job working for a top oil company. Keith convinced Viola that working for "the enemy" was a good decision because, in order to change the energy industry, reform needed to start from within. Keith assured Viola that his dreams hadn't changed. He still dreamed of a carbon-neutral, healthy world for their daughter. But he truly believed that he could have a bigger impact working from the inside. *After all,* he reasoned, *if this big oil company, and dozens of others, are the cause of so much pollution, they could also be the solution. These companies have the power and means to change things.* He imagined that he could help steer the company's business model away from fossil fuels and towards renewable energy sources— like wind, solar, and geothermal—because renewables are much more profitable in the long term. Mostly because with renewables, a person can think long term.

Soon after Keith started that job, he realized his ideas of getting the company to pursue renewable energy sources would need to be put on hold, because he didn't have enough experience to be listened to yet. He decided to play the "long game," so he could earn his co-workers' respect to get their support. But after working with the same people for years, these oil guys and gals became his friends. His moral compass, which had previously been black and white, became completely gray. He knew these people's spouses and kids. They had wonderful senses of humor, and they were overall nice people with good hearts. The longer he stayed in the business, the more loyal he became to his colleagues. He shied away from making the sweeping changes he'd dreamed of because he knew how unpopular both he and the changes would be.

And, he wasn't going to lie. Keith loved the luxury. After he transitioned to being a lobbyist, he made a fine living. He grew up in apartments and mobile homes, eating cheap, highly processed food. Now he had become accustomed to having whatever he wanted, whenever he wanted, however he wanted it, wherever he wanted it.

Although he always admired Viola, who consistently took the high road and saw the best in others, their lives had drifted apart. He *didn't* always see the good in people like she did. In fact, Keith reveled in laughing at people's stupidity, and he understood the thrill of living a little outside the law. Besides their daughter, he and Viola had little in common. That's when Viola and Keith filed for divorce, citing irreconcilable differences as the cause.

But when he and his wife divorced, Ivy only got to visit him on weekends. On top of that, too many of those weekends were shortened since he often needed to fly out on Sundays in order to be in D.C. early on Monday mornings.

Keith and his daughter grew apart. His life in the city was entirely different than her life in the suburbs, and when Ivy would come to the city to stay with him, he could tell that she didn't feel at home there. She was more comfortable in her routine with her mom. He also knew that Ivy didn't like his girlfriends because she never bothered learning their names.

Salomon interrupted Keith's thoughts and escorted him to a series of massive control panels with hundreds of labeled sliders.

"Now, Keith," he said, "it is your job to use these controls to figure out how to move forward. What is done is done. There is no going back. But, there is a future. That is, there is a future if you make the right choices for the planet and humanity. The sliders you see in front of you control a detailed, simulated world. The sliders aren't actually controlling the world, so move them around as much as you'd like."

Salomon's slow and steady voice narrated, "Global temperatures will continue to rise for decades because of the pollution that has already been created. The question is, how much will the temperatures continue to rise—by two degrees or ten degrees? Society and environmental systems will likely adapt to a couple of degrees—but remember, the planet was only five to nine degrees Fahrenhiet colder during the last ice age. There is just no way humans and animals can evolve quickly enough to handle this radical change. We need to hold the overall temperature change within 2.7 °F. Right now, we are on course for a 7.3 °F increase within eighty years." [16]

Only eighty years? If things don't change, Ivy won't even have a chance to live a full life and die of old age, realized Keith. He got right to work adjusting the levers trying every alternative. He found that in a future where heat-trapping gas emissions continued to grow, frost-free growing seasons increased in the U.S. by about a month. At first, he thought this could be advantageous, but he quickly saw the drought, wildfires, and everything else he had just witnessed on his tour followed soon after. He ran different scenarios using the climate change simulator to adjust hundreds of factors—energy supplies, transportation systems, land uses, population growth, industry emissions, carbon taxes, carbon removal tactics, and more. He worked for hours without looking up or taking a break. He'd always had the ability to over-focus on projects and lose track of time, but this project was unlike anything he'd ever done.

A clear path to "stop the bleeding"—as his Defender had said— became obvious. Implementing a large carbon tax and reinvesting that money in energy efficiency and electrification supplied by renewables would limit the global temperature to 3.2 °F.[17] *That's 84% of our planetary goal of holding the temperature at 2.7 °F. It's a no-brainer.* He told Salomon, "I'm ready."

CHAPTER 5

Camaraderie

After their tours, the Ejected were all dropped—like bombs—in the same realm where they first met. They were haggard, hungry, and horrified. No one talked or could look each other in the eye. They all knew they were responsible for so many ills on Earth. Even if they weren't directly responsible for certain actions or problems, they knew that they hadn't done everything in their power to do the right thing for the planet or for the good of humanity.

Seth brought the Ejected together and summarized what everyone had learned on their various tours. "Human activities have already warmed the planet about 1.8 °F since the pre-industrial era, around 1850,"[18] he announced. "At the current rate of warming, the Earth's average temperature will rise another 0.9 °F and reach the maximum livable temperature increase between 2030 and 2052. Limiting the total warming requires drastic changes."

He looked at each of the Ejected as he explained, "You all have learned different ways to reduce our carbon dioxide equivalents—often called CO_2e for short—and we need every strategy implemented in order to have a chance of survival and for you to have a chance of returning to your families. No one will be able to return to Earth until enough emissions are reduced to support you all. Also, because CO_2

remains in the atmosphere for centuries, temperatures will continue to rise," he continued. "As a result, even with drastic emission cuts, meeting this 2.7 °F goal likely means that the Earth will go over the 2.7 °F threshold for a time before returning to a more livable level for the longer term.[19] We need to follow the Paris Climate Change Agreement's guidelines to the full extent. That's why we also need some removal of CO_2 from the atmosphere by reforestation, soil carbon sequestration, or other technological advancements. In short, net carbon dioxide equivalent emissions need to drop forty-five percent from their 2010 levels by 2030, and reach net zero by 2050. To keep the math simple, and to err on the side of caution, let's say we need to cut global emissions in half."

"What does 'net zero' mean?" asked the lady with the pearls.

Keith smirked as he recalled how this lady had bragged about her brainy Ph.D. *How's that fancy Ph.D. working for you now?* wondered Keith. He couldn't help it. He loved silently picking on people he found annoying.

"'Net zero' means offsetting any remaining CO_2e emissions by removing CO_2e from the atmosphere," explained Aziza.

The lady stared blankly as if no explanation had been given. Keith watched this self-proclaimed genius with amusement.

Recognizing that this lady wasn't tracking, Aziza continued, "Imagine a bathtub with the faucet running. To keep the tub from overflowing, you can either turn off the running water or unplug the drain, right?"

Lady Einstein nodded.

"Turning off the water faucet is like reducing emissions because it's stopping the emissions at their sources. Opening the drain is like finding carbon sinks—like trees, soil, or oceans—that store the carbon and sort of "drain" them out of the atmosphere."

The lady nodded at Aziza very slowly, which convinced Keith that she still didn't get it.

One of the Ejected stood up and began to speak, "The world will go on, but the question is, will people? We are destroying the resources that give us life—the air, water, and land." This man was thin, but not frail. His voice was quiet, calm, and even and his eyes were warm and wise. Just being in his presence felt like an honor. Everyone waited for him to continue, "I learned on my tour that the fossil fuels that are currently powering most aspects of the world are killing millions of people every year. And they have been for decades. Our collective lack of a reaction doesn't make sense. It doesn't mirror the problem that is at hand. I've always thought God will take care of us. But it is clear to me that we need to do our part and not stand by idly. We have a crisis on our hands, and we all need to solve this so we can go back to our families."

A sense of unity swept across the Ejected, and this man's speech was met with applause.

Another Ejected stood up and declared, "We need to turn the page on greed and apathy and look toward love and light to find generosity and concern, compassion, and commitment to all do our part."

A loud voice from the back chimed in with, "Community and health!"

"We need to hold hands with our neighbors and find a way to connect with and help each other. We need to put away the blame and judgment because we all use our planet's resources, and no one is guilt free. We just don't know everyone's story, so we must practice restraint in judging others."

Yet another of the Ejected, who was caught up in the emotion, yelled, "Because we won't do better until we all do better!"

One by one, the Ejected stepped up and announced how many gigatons of emissions they thought they could reduce and what percentage that would be of the total. It was clear to everyone, without even exchanging words, that there would be winners and losers in people's jobs for the short term, but that collectively, humans would be the biggest losers if drastic changes weren't made immediately. The path forward was clear: reduce energy needs and overall consumption of all resources and quickly transition away from fossil fuels to renewables. The big picture wasn't complicated.

It was a race against time to save humanity. Could these historically selfish, sorry souls actually save their species?

CHAPTER 6

Surprise Visit

It had been a few hours now, and her dad still hadn't picked her up from her mom's house. Her mom had left for the weekend for a yoga retreat because it was Ivy's weekend to be with her dad. Ivy stomped around the house because nothing was going her way. She thought it would be awesome to be by herself and have unlimited screen time, but technology seemed to have gone on strike. Her fingerprint I.D. wouldn't work and her password didn't work either. She tried the password again: DaddysG1rl!. She had to laugh. Her dad had created the password, and she secretly liked it, although she'd never admit that to him. Then she noticed that the Wi-Fi network didn't show up. Next, her computer said it was out of hard drive space, and she couldn't get a signal on her cell phone.

She looked out the window and let the setting sun shine on her face. She loved that days were so long in the northern hemisphere at the end of May. It was almost 9:00 p.m., and it was still light! It was a nice evening, and it would've been nice to walk around Grand Avenue and get pizza and ice cream like they were supposed to tonight. Or go for a motorcycle ride. Now she was feeling bad about thinking she didn't want to see her dad. She really did. She knew she was Daddy's girl. She always would be. She and her dad had the same sense of humor and the same drive and determination. Although she shared many things with her mom, their relationship was just… different. Her mom was content and calm. Ivy made things happen, just like her dad. She had an adventurous spirit and wasn't afraid to take risks.

She looked around the house at the battlefield of uncooperative electronic devices and decided that it seemed like the universe was giving her some sort of signal to use less energy or something. She made herself a sandwich and followed it with an indulgent pint of ice cream. Then she read a paperback book and went to bed.

***

In the morning, Ivy woke up to a quiet house, so she flipped on the TV for some company. At least that still works, she thought.

A special report interrupted her program to announce that police stations were being flooded with missing persons reports. As she processed the information, her eyes widened and her jaw dropped involuntarily. Could it be that her dad was one of these people who had mysteriously disappeared? Her gut told her yes, because her dad was never late. Plus, her dad would never not call to tell her what was keeping him if he was late. He was Mr. Dependable.

Ivy called her dad's phone for the millionth time. He still didn't pick up, just got his stupid voicemail. Her thoughts were interrupted by a tapping sound on her window that sounded like hail hitting it. It was a beautiful morning, so it couldn't be hail. As she went over to the second story window to examine, she witnessed pebbles hitting the window, over and over. Where were they coming from? Ivy looked around to see if it was windy, but the tree branches weren't swaying. "Why are these rocks hitting my window?" she asked herself aloud.

Over and over, the same rhythm. Tap, tap, tap, tap. Slight pause. Tap, tap. Again. Tap, tap, tap, tap. Pause. Tap, tap. A third time. Ivy walked away and popped some bread in the toaster. The rhythm echoed in her head. Why did that pattern seem so familiar?

And then she recognized it. That's how her dad knocked on her bedroom door every morning to wake her up. He said it was Morse code. He had learned Morse code as a kid and thought she should, too. *Could it be that Dad is trying to communicate with me?* She searched 'Morse code' online. *Yay! The internet is working!* She found a YouTube video titled "How to Learn Morse Code Alphabet in 3 Steps."

She played the video and stopped it at the display of a Morse code chart. She learned four taps was "H." Pauses were between letters, and the second "tap, tap" was "I." H-I. She knocked "Hi" back on the window. Then she knocked long, short, short. Pause. Short, long. Pause. Long, short, short, spelling "dad," and raised her shoulders as though she were asking a question. He tapped "yes" back.

"Where are you?" tapped Ivy.

No reply. Keith was at a loss to explain where he was with a few taps.

"Are you OK?" she tapped.

"Yes," he answered.

Still in her pajamas, Ivy ran outside to find her dad. She called for him frantically, but there was no answer. She began to cry. This was really freaking her out and she wondered if she was imagining the whole thing.

Suddenly knocking came from the picnic table. She searched for him but saw nothing. She ran over to the table and started grasping at the air to see if she could touch him. But she couldn't. She jumped up onto the table and occupied as much space as she could to see if she could find him, crying all the while. She heard more tapping but then realized she didn't have her Morse code cheat sheet with her, so she announced that she was grabbing it as she ran in. She returned with paper and a pen and her tablet. She said, "I'm ready, Dad." She hoped that he hadn't disappeared—again.

"Can you hear me?" she called out. She was relieved to hear a series of knocks that spelled yes. Then she then started firing off questions, like *Why can't I hear or see you?* His response was an unsatisfying *'I don't know.'* She listened to the taps and transcribed his messages for the rest of the morning, until the sun came around the house and made it too hot to be outside at the table.

Ivy learned that people have about ten years to cut carbon emissions in half and that he couldn't return to Earth until greenhouse gas levels were brought down to 2010 levels. Ivy wanted to ask him what he thought she and her mom—and Greta Thunberg—had been saying for the last several years, but she decided that wouldn't be helpful, and it wouldn't bring him back any sooner. She mostly just wanted to know how she could help secure his return.

Ivy's dad explained that he wanted her to use her social media influence to make adopting a sustainable lifestyle mainstream. She never dreamed her fourteen-year-old voice could influence anything, but now that she thought about it, thanks to a silly but socially relevant video of hers going viral, she now had a wildly popular YouTube channel with millions of subscribers. She'd made most of the videos rather spontaneously without a script or a lot of editing. Somehow her quirky style and messages resonated with a broad base of people. Ivy agreed to help do this, but she argued that her efforts would never be enough.

Her dad recognized this fact and communicated that he had other plans too, and that there were thousands of what he called 'Ejected' people working to meet this goal as well. He assured her that the weight of the world and his return did not rest solely on her shoulders. He just wanted her to do her best. She again agreed to do whatever she could.

Tears stinging her eyes, Ivy said, "I want to hug you, but there's nothing to hug."

She felt a warmth on her cheek that she knew must have been his kiss.

Keith tapped, 'Bye 4 now I luv u.'

Ivy sat at the picnic table, stunned for a couple of minutes as she tried to process what was happening. But she quickly decided that time was of the essence, so she ran inside to get to work.

CHAPTER 7

The Blueprint

Ivy already knew quite a bit about environmental issues. Since her mom worked in the renewable energy industry, Ivy had grown up discussing carbon dioxide equivalents, alternating current, and gigawatts at the dinner table. She went to work researching sustainable lifestyles in her mom's sunny and spacious office. It was a wonderful space to spend time, with large windows on three sides and French doors that connected to the kitchen on the fourth side. Best of all, the windows looked out onto native gardens that hummed with pollinator activity. Ivy's mom always said she never had to work a day in her life because she was passionate about her job. And it never really felt like work—especially when she got to spend her days in such a lovely environment.

First, Ivy needed to figure out what the end goal was and what "sustainable" meant. She had an inkling already that the U.S. and China were the largest greenhouse gas emitters. She searched several reputable websites that had similar information, but the graph on the Union of Concerned Scientists website made it crystal clear that the weight was definitely on the shoulders of China and the U.S. to reduce emissions. China was responsible for about twenty-eight percent of the world's emissions, and the U.S., for fourteen percent. Just two countries are responsible for nearly half of the planet's greenhouse gas emissions.[20] *That's disgusting,* she thought.

She dug deeper and found out that the U.S. had contributed the most global CO_2 emissions overall—about 25 percent of the world's total emissions to date.[21] *Great*, thought Ivy, *the U.S. is the biggest carbon dioxide polluter in history, and we are home to only 4.25 percent of the world's population.*[22] *That's not just disgusting, that's immoral.*

She was hoping that this information was wrong, so she kept searching. Unfortunately, she kept finding similar numbers. She also found that the average Chinese person contributes a relatively modest 7.5 metric tons of CO_2e per year, whereas the average person in the U.S. contributes a sickening 16.5 metric tons.[23] She saw other figures that estimated Americans contribute as high as 28 metric tons per person. She hoped that was wrong. From what she could find, the global average seemed to be about 4.5 metric tons of CO_2 per person each year.[24]

Her dad said that "we" needed to cut emissions in half. But how does that work? Should everyone on Earth reduce their footprints by half? She wished she would've asked her dad that question. Some countries barely contribute any greenhouse gas emissions to start with. Or maybe the biggest polluters should reduce their footprints by more than half so everyone is on a more level playing field? After some thought, she decided that the second option would be the right thing to do. Americans should feel duty bound to cut their egregious levels by more than half, since they are so much higher already.

Next, Ivy looked into where the emissions were coming from. She looked by economic sectors first, but didn't know how that translated to individuals, so she found information about where the average American's carbon emissions were coming from. She found that:

1. Home energy use was 32%, with over half (17%) for heating and cooling
2. Transportation, with gas-powered vehicles accounts for about 28%
3. Stuff we buy is 26%
4. Food is 14%[25]

Average American's Carbon Emissions

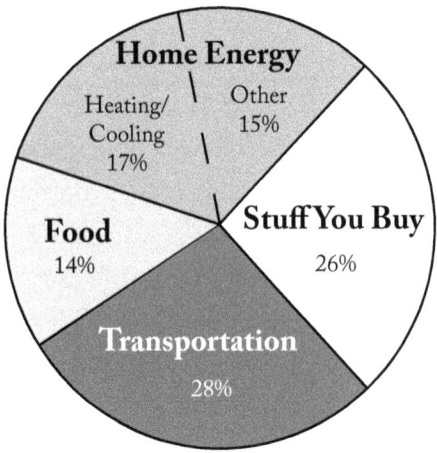

This list seemed pretty straightforward, so she started a new Google doc and brainstormed a list of ways to bring down the consumption in each area.

Zeroing Out Home Energy Use

-17% Heating and Cooling

"To eliminate the need for heating and cooling systems, we need more passive buildings," muttered Ivy to herself. Ivy knew a little about hyper-insulated "passive" houses, because she lived in one with her mom. Visitors were typically shocked to find out they didn't have—or even need—a furnace or an air conditioner despite living in their extreme Midwest climate where annual temperature differences can span a hundred degrees. She and her mom also had rooftop solar, so they consumed no energy from the grid and actually sold their excess energy back to the local energy company. She knew that building passive houses costs more upfront because they have thicker walls and

way better windows, but they paid for themselves in energy savings. *Now let's look at the remaining fifteen percent of the energy used in homes.*

-15 % Misc.

The biggest home energy uses are water heaters, lighting, and inefficient appliances. *Reducing energy consumption wherever possible would be the first thing to do by installing LED lighting and more efficient appliances,* thought Ivy. Then the rest of the energy use could be supplied by renewables.

Implementing passive building design, energy efficiency, and renewable energy could essentially zero out the home energy use sector. Of course, renewable energy sources have a footprint to build and install, but in the long term, and certainly in comparison with coal, the impact is minimal.

OK, Ivy thought, *this isn't so hard. Why don't adults sit down and solve the climate crisis? It's obvious that the solutions exist. So, adults just don't think the future is worth protecting? Or all they care about is making money at the future's expense? Or they can't stop arguing about inconsequential details and get over their egos to do something for the common good?* Ivy didn't understand adults and how illogical they are. She felt the climate crisis was like everyone's house was on fire, and all of the adults were still sitting on the couch eating potato chips watching their favorite show, not bothering to evacuate or call 911.

Tackling the 28% from Transportation

Ivy was a born list maker, so she started with what came naturally to her by making another one.

- Reduce need for transportation by slowing down the pace of life, using video conferencing, working from home.
- Switch to electric vehicles, add a *lot* of charging stations to

make it convenient for people.
- Make communities more walkable and bike-able.
- Promote carpools and hourly electric car rental systems.
- Build mass transit
- Eat food that is locally grown.

Ivy wondered if this last item should be in this transportation category or in the food category. She figured she might as well put it in both since it fits in both.

Well, look at this, Ivy thought as a tiny smile appeared for an instant, *this area could also practically be zeroed out, too.*

To use stuff and eat food is essential for survival, so we are clearly not getting this forty percent of the carbon footprint to zero. But, we can do a lot better than we are. She couldn't find exact numbers for these items, and it would never be the same for each individual, but she found various online carbon footprint calculators and found out that most people could probably cut their footprints in half without compromising their comfortable lifestyle and modern conveniences.

Ivy recognized that this area was going to look different for everyone. *The main thing is, since we cannot tackle such massive problems alone, everyone needs to do what they can in whatever way they can.* She knew there needed to be tolerance of different ways of going about things. Different people have different needs and skills, after all. For example, a person who needs to be gluten and dairy-free might need to eat quite a bit of meat, which generally has a larger carbon footprint. That's fine. A person with a special medical need might use a whole lot of plastic medical supplies to aid with his or her condition. Of course, plastics in life-saving medical supplies and devices had to be seen as a free pass. No one was going to fault a person for needing to use inhalers, sterile tubing, or a pacemaker with plastic components. Again, all totally necessary. It would have to be up to people to do their very best and for other people not to pass judgment on others. That was the tricky part. It's so easy to pass judgment.

Ivy recognized that many people around the world don't have their basic needs met and could never make the decisions to live a more environmentally conscious life without support, because they are just trying to survive however they can. She thought about a Mexican village she and her extended family had visited while on vacation. After visiting some local 4,000-year-old petroglyphs, her family had eaten lunch in a tiny village about an hour outside of Mazatlán, where they got to know a few of the villagers. Ana was the village teacher and had helped prepare their meal over a wood-fire stove. Whereas the tortillas tasted amazing cooked that way, Ivy recognized it wasn't the healthiest for the air and for Ana and the other women cooking on the stove breathing in all that soot. There also weren't many trees around, so it didn't seem like it would be very easy to find sustainably-sourced wood for the stove. But what other stove choice did they have?

Ivy's youngest cousin, Sam, befriended Ana's son Santiago. They were both seven years old, and it didn't take long for the two seven-year-old boys to go off and play together. When Ivy found them playing at Santiago's house, she noted that the family owned about as much stuff as her family traveled with. She was ashamed that just her mom's house alone had more in storage than this family had in their entire house. Then there was her dad's house, which was full of stuff, too.

Ivy quickly decided that her lifestyle influencing wasn't going to be directed to people who weren't in the economic position to make long-term decisions that were best for sustainability. Her aim was to reach the people who had the ability to make those decisions—and knew it was the right thing to do—but chose not to live more simply because they just didn't want to be inconvenienced.

Cutting Stuff in Half

The goal would be to reduce consumption by half, bringing the CO_2e footprint to around thirteen percent. Of course, this would be accomplished by reducing consumption first, reusing next, and recycling if nothing else can be done with an item. *Voluntary simplicity—or living a simpler life not centered on possessions—would be key to move the needle on reducing the stuff in people's lives.*

Ivy reflected on the steps her grandma always walked her through before Ivy made a purchase with the birthday money she would get from her grandma. "Do you really need it?" Grandma Ethel would ask, "Could it be borrowed, rented, or purchased secondhand instead?" Then Grandma would also ask probing questions like where it was made and how far was it shipped to get to her. Were the materials used sustainable? Was the product or toy durable? How long would she use it? Could it be recycled?

This line of questioning talked Ivy out of buying many fad toys. Her grandma never actually told Ivy what to do; she would just ask Ivy these questions before they got to the check-out register. It seemed that nine times out of ten, Ivy would decide that she either didn't need the cheaply made toy or that she could get it used.

Food Footprints

As with the "stuff" category, Ivy's goal was also to cut this in half— not by eating half of the calories, but by reducing packaging and "food miles."

- Cook your own meals based on locally-grown, seasonal food to minimize "food miles"
- Eat less processed or packaged food
- Eat a more plant-based diet whenever possible. Just changing from a meat-lover diet to a no-beef diet nearly cuts greenhouse gas emissions in half.
- Avoid ruminant animals, like sheep and cows, because their multiple stomachs and the way they process their food makes their methane contribution crazy high.

Ivy thought this fact was a little funny. Cow and sheep farts are actually a serious planetary problem! Sustainably raised fish, poultry, and even pork have much lower footprints.

Something Ivy found super interesting is that local pork had a lower footprint than an American vegan's jackfruit shipped from Asia. She determined that it was less about what a person ate (you don't need to be a vegan) and more about where their food comes from.

Whoa, she thought. She re-added the totals and realized this scenario would reduce CO_2e footprints by eighty percent and bring footprints to nearer to a 3.3-ton lifestyle, instead of a 16.5-ton lifestyle. Making a short list for each of the four items made solving the climate crisis seem manageable. *It's not rocket science. Why are people acting like this is such a mysterious problem to solve?* She had a plan, but how was she going to get people to go along with the it?

Ivy looked at the clock in the corner of her computer screen and realized that it was 5:00 p.m. No wonder she was starving. She'd never even eaten the toast she'd put in the toaster that morning, and she was still in her pajamas. Light-headed from hunger, Ivy went to the kitchen, opened the fridge, and searched for food that didn't require preparation. Quick was pretty much her only criteria. She gobbled down cold leftover vegetarian lasagna, followed by grapes, a hard-boiled egg, and crackers by the handful from the pantry closet. Crumbs flew everywhere as she shoved them into her mouth.

Ivy contemplated her plan of action as her blood sugar stabilized. She decided that instead of tackling individual behaviors and a giant list of "101 things you can do to reduce your footprint," it was time to bring about a cultural and moral revolution where people bonded and acknowledged the peril they were in together instead of just ignoring it. *In order to get people to work together,* she thought, *we need to heal the division in our country. People need to feel accepted by the other side. And we all need to stop taking sides. We are one humanity that needs to unite against a common threat. That's a pretty tall order for a 14-year old,* she thought, *I need Jayla.*

She texted her best friend, Jayla, who lived three doors down, and asked her to come over ASAP. Jayla and Ivy had met in pre-school, when they traded pastel-colored marshmallows for pastel-colored dinner mints at snack time. They both vividly remembered this calculated trade that sealed their friendship and they'd been inseparable ever since.

Ivy barely put her phone down before Jayla knocked and then let herself in, like she always did. Even though Jayla knew everything about her, Ivy was a little nervous that Jayla wouldn't believe that her father had appeared to her as a pebble-throwing ghost, then communicated with her through Morse code to tell her she needed to help save humanity by changing consumptive culture. It was more than a little out there! Ivy recognized that she'd have a hard time believing the story if she heard it from someone else, but if there was anyone in the world that might believe her, it was Jayla.

Jayla was super smart, not just book smart—although she was that too—but also intuitive and wise. Ivy called her an old soul because she always seemed to know what to do in any situation and seemed wise beyond her fourteen years of age. One time when they were swimming at a crowded beach, and the lifeguard hadn't noticed their friend Kris flailing because the area around the bulkhead was so crowded, Jayla jumped in, brought Kris to shore, and calmly cleared her airways. It was as if saving drowning victims' lives was something she did every week. Ivy remembered that she'd just stood on the bulkhead, frozen in terror. Yes, there was certainly much more to Jayla than met the eye. She wasn't just a skinny kid. She was a brilliant hero. She always felt a little awe-struck by her and felt blessed to be able to call her not only a friend, but her *best* friend.

"Hey, Jay," said Ivy as she greeted Jayla at the top of the stairs. They gave each other a quick hug and Jayla perched herself on the edge of the kitchen stool and asked, "What's up? I thought you were with your dad this weekend."

Ivy nodded and dove right in, explaining everything so fast that only a best friend like Jayla could keep up. She started with the fact that her dad had never showed up to pick her up. Shocked at this news, Jayla's already enormous brown eyes widened. Jayla knew Keith was never late, and that this was super worrisome. She didn't blink and hung on every word. Ivy asked if Jayla had heard the news that people around the world had disappeared. Jayla nodded, with an expression that said, "duh" and replied that it's all over the news and social media right now. Ivy then explained the whole encounter with her dad, that he was one of the missing people, and what he'd told her to do. Jayla didn't question whether Ivy was telling the truth, but just asked Ivy what her plan was to get him back.

Ivy walked Jayla through her research and explained that her goal was to make a 3.3-ton CO_2e lifestyle the norm. Jayla suggested that Ivy should keep it simple and stick with 3 rather than 3.3, because 3.3 didn't roll off the tongue quite as nicely. S-he added that three was a great number to use because it was kind of a magical number representing the past, present, and future; faith, hope, and charity; mind, body, and soul; the holy trinity; birth, life, and death; the beginning, middle, and end, and so on. Ivy was baffled by how Jayla could just rattle that knowledge off without hesitation.

Jayla pointed out that bringing the number down to three was reducing the American carbon footprint by a little over eighty percent, but she agreed with Ivy that Americans should finally set a good example of what was possible—especially since Americans were, per person, the Earth's biggest culprits for environmental destruction. She also pointed out that many environmentally-friendly lifestyle choices were expensive and that not everyone could afford to switch—at least not without some help.

Then Jayla proceeded to school Ivy about environmental justice. Now it was Ivy's turn to listen intently. Jayla explained, "Environmental justice is about treating all people fairly and involving all people in developing, implementing, and enforcing environmental laws. Currently black and brown-skinned people are much more likely to live in polluted neighborhoods and their rates of asthma and a bunch of cancers are much higher because of this pollution."

Stunned, Ivy asked, "Why?"

And Jayla responded in typical Jayla fashion with facts and references, "The EPA's National Center for Environmental Assessment released a study showing that people of color were much more likely to live near polluters and breathe polluted air. Specifically, people in poverty were exposed to more fine particulate matter than people living above poverty—and this is at national, state, and county levels.[26]

"Where is all that fine particulate matter coming from, Jay?" asked Ivy.

"Like car fumes, smog, soot, oil smoke, ash, and construction dust," Jayla explained, "and polluters and pollution are disproportionately located in communities of color. It's kind of hard to prove, but it seems pretty intentional that so many hazardous waste landfills, coal-burning power plants and hydraulic-fracturing oil wells end up in black and poor neighborhoods."

Ivy was utterly horrified to learn this appalling information. This calculated racism made her feel despondent, and, once again, ashamed to be white. Yet another example of white people acting like black lives don't matter. It was incomprehensible to Ivy. Jayla was Black and she meant the world to Ivy. How could anyone ever say people with a certain attribute deserve to be ill-treated? *It's revolting. It's sinful. It's inexcusable. It needs to change. Now.* She wondered how this behavior could continue and how the people in power who were responsible could live with themselves.

Ivy recognized that even though Jayla was like a sister to her, and she felt like they were practically one, they lived in separate worlds. Never once was Ivy followed around a store with a watchful eye that assumed she might steal something, but Jayla was. Ivy had witnessed it at the drug-store on the corner. That owner had followed Jayla around like an eagle after a mouse as if Jayla would surely steal if she weren't watched. Seeing the whole charade made Ivy want to pop some stuff into her pocket just so the shopkeeper would rethink her stereotypes. But she didn't have the nerve to steal anything. When Ivy joined Jayla in the makeup aisle, the worker magically drifted away. Ivy told Jayla she noticed that lady was watching her. Jayla said, "Yeah, I knew it too. Did you see how I was making that dumb lady run all through the store? That's more exercise than that lady has gotten all week!"

Jayla also told Ivy that her dad had been pulled over multiple times and questioned whether the car he was driving belonged to him.

Ivy asked naively, "Why would the cop wonder that?"

Jayla replied, "Because the officer didn't expect to see a Black man in an Audi."

Dumb-founded, Ivy shouted, "WHAAAAAT? Your dad is an engineer! Why wouldn't he be driving a nice car?"

"Right?" Jayla asked rhetorically.

The kicker was that Jayla told Ivy that once a cop questioned her whether she was riding with "this man" voluntarily. At first, Jayla didn't even realize what the cop was getting at. But she soon realized that the cop thought "this man" might be kidnapping her or something. In response to this insane racial profiling, Jayla had lost it and started screaming at the officer that this was her *dad* and they were going to a swim meet. Thanks to him, they were going to be late and she'd miss her spot in the starting lineup.

Ivy agreed with Jayla that they absolutely needed to make environmental justice the basis of their sustainability plan.

CHAPTER 8

Stop the Bleeding

Keith learned on his tour that being one of the Ejected gave him the ability to travel anywhere, but he was still figuring out the details of how to be visible or invisible and heard or muted. Keith decided he should practice since he clearly didn't have the settings optimized when he visited Ivy.

Keith reviewed his plan. The National Green Energy Policy bill had gone through the House and the Senate and was waiting to be signed into law by the president. He was going to sneak into the Government Printing Office that night and revise this energy policy to include a carbon tax. He needed to make sure he had the settings correct before then.

He looked around for Salomon or one of the other Ejected to help him figure out the settings in the realm, but he didn't see anyone, so he decided he'd try to figure it out himself. He cautiously entered the control panel room and read the settings aloud to himself, "Location. Hmm. I've always wanted to visit the Eiffel Tower." So, he typed in *Eiffel Tower, Paris, France.*

"Auto-think location," read Keith next. "That sounds handy. Let's go with that," and he turned that setting on. The next setting was "Visible." Under this setting, there were scores of other settings. Since he wasn't quite sure what they did, he decided to just switch them all on. Then he closed his eyes and envisioned standing beneath the Eiffel Tower.

When he opened his eyes, he was thrilled to see the Eiffel Tower in front of him. He started to turn in a circle so he could take it all in. As he made a quarter turn, he realized that he must be visible because people were watching him, and they looked as excited as he was. He beamed at the crowd who couldn't seem to take their eyes off him and proudly used his limited French to cheerfully say, "Bonjour!" to the people who were within earshot. As he gazed at the Eiffel Tower, he felt so alive that his skin tingled.

Suddenly, his elation turned to horror as he realized why his skin felt so tingly and why he was Mr. Popular. Somehow, Keith had transported himself *sans* clothing. Naked as a newborn, he stood beneath the most romantic icon in the world like some creepy exhibitionist.

He searched for a place to hide, but there were people in every direction. Throughout his life, he'd had a recurring nightmare that he would show up on the first day of school without clothes on. Only this time he wasn't dreaming. He was actually naked in France!

He knew all he had to do was think of another location to get out of there since he had the "Auto-Think Location" setting turned on, so he closed his eyes and wished to be anywhere else. Apparently "anywhere" wasn't specific enough because he remained beneath the symbol of love, drawing a growing, curious crowd that opted to stay a safe distance away.

All his panicked brain could think was, *Oh, my God, oh, my God, oh, my God! School nightmare, school nightmare, school nightmare!* Apparently, that was enough to transport him to Roosevelt Senior High. Fortunately, it was evening, so there weren't people around to see his naked self. His mind was a little clearer now, and he realized that where he needed to go was back to the control room to figure out the sub-settings under appearance.

As Keith paced around the realm trying to calm himself, he recognized that he knew all of the arguments about why a carbon tax supposedly wasn't good for the world, but he also knew that all of those arguments were deliberate deceptions motivated by greed. *Since over eighty percent of U.S. energy consumption comes from natural gas, oil, and coal,*[27] *the fossil fuels industry has it in their best interest to keep the country hooked,* thought Keith.

Keith figured out using the model on his tour that a well-designed carbon tax could capture about ninety percent of U.S. emissions by taxing only several thousand taxpayers who could easily afford it.[28] *It's beautiful. This way, the carbon tax doesn't increase the cost of goods and services because the higher energy prices wouldn't need to be passed on to consumers.* But, even if prices increased, he didn't see it as a negative outcome anymore. The increase would push markets and consumers to reduce their consumption, find alternatives and support renewables very quickly.

Keith reflected on how he used to argue that carbon taxes weren't a "market-driven solution," but he'd known all along that the true cost to the planet of extracting resources from the Earth, as well as the cost of shipping, processing, and the burning of fossil fuels, wasn't being accounted for. Adding a carbon tax to reflect how much of an impact fossil fuels have on the world would be justice finally being served. It's true that a few of his friends would lose a bit of money, but the smart ones would see the truth and invest in renewables. The fossil fuel industry is most definitely a huge problem, but it could also be the solution if they were to use their power for good. He had always thought that.

An argument that Keith knew was full of holes was that a carbon tax would damage American economic competitiveness by making it too expensive for companies to produce in this country. *But, in reality,* thought Keith, *if we ruin our natural resources—upon which our personal health and economy are completely dependent—and live the nightmare I just experienced on the tour, that will be much worse for business.*

Even if it did take the rest of the world a while to transition to a renewable economy, everyone would be forced to do so. *Plus, if we propose border taxes for imports from countries without a carbon tax,* Keith thought, *that should take care of the economic competitiveness problem.*

He decided that he wanted to be invisible and have his voice turned off so he didn't accidentally cough or anything. After playing cupid in France without even the dignity of a diaper, Keith sought out Salomon to help him with his settings. Salomon also helped him figure out the building access logistics and accompanied him on the journey. They waited for nightfall so the Government Printing Office would be empty.

They successfully revised the energy bill to include an enormous carbon tax and also composed job transition plans so workers employed in fossil fuel industries could be retrained into clean energy jobs. He made the language clear that the revenue from the carbon taxes would be used for reducing greenhouse gases through energy conservation and creating clean energy infrastructure that included solar, wind, and geothermal energy sources, as well as car-charging stations spread across the country. Finally, the climate crisis was declared a national emergency which required nationwide mobilization to fight—similar to the WWII war effort.

Luckily, this president isn't big on reading, thought Keith. He knew this president would just rely on an aide to tell him whether he should sign it. *The aide will think she knows what's in the bill, so she will advise him to move forward with it.*

And so, it came to pass. A carbon tax was quietly slipped into law. No lawmakers complained because they didn't want to admit that they hadn't read the bill and didn't know the carbon tax was in it. The carbon tax law took effect the next day. To the legislators' surprise, the voters were in favor of the carbon tax. There was a refreshing feeling of solidarity to get the Ejected back home and most people realized that a carbon tax would help achieve this goal. So, lawmakers on both sides of the aisle claimed victory. It was beautiful.

CHAPTER 9

Live Simply

"Live simply so others may simply live."
—Mahatma Gandhi

Ivy and Jayla were hard at work building a robust social media campaign to promote sustainability that started with environmental justice. Ivy was still hungry, so she asked Jayla if she wanted to order pizza.

Jayla asked with a huge smile, "Have I *ever* said no to pizza?"

Ivy giggled. She knew her skinny friend could put away impressive quantities of pizza and had been known to out-eat beefy football players when it came to pizza.

They ordered it and sat on the deck eating as the filtered light from the honey locust tree danced across their faces. As Ivy and Jayla imagined what this three-ton CO_2e-per-year lifestyle would look like, Ivy suggested that the pace of life needed to slow down, a lot. She brought up the beginning of COVID times and how everyone was forced to stay home and slow down. The culture changed overnight when there was a direct threat to people. The threat of spreading the virus united most people's actions.

"Ironically," said Ivy, "there has been a direct threat to humans for over three decades. And the climate crisis has been killing thousands of people each day through direct and indirect impacts, yet the situation is essentially still being ignored."

Jayla surmised, "Perhaps there is no unity because there is no plan."

Ivy said, "Yeah, and there isn't a plan because people are too short-sighted to realize they need a plan."

Ivy and Jayla recollected about the beginning of COVID. Online school was much shorter and video conferencing became a major thing overnight—even preschool classes were using Zoom. They had learned that video conferencing platforms were a decent substitute for meetings, piano lessons, social gatherings, and even concerts on TV. A lot of people also found they could work from home pretty effectively if they had a decent computer and internet connection. Some people preferred not going to an office and resolved never to go back to engaging in so many in-person meetings again.

For many people with desk jobs, it was a gift to eliminate long commutes. People had time to sleep in, cook their own meals, and exercise. *Ironically, despite the global pandemic that tragically cost so many lives,* thought Ivy, *some nonessential workers experienced better health from eating right, exercising, sleeping more, and practicing gratitude.* People had seemed more centered and had kept their eye on the things that really mattered: their health and loved ones.

Jayla told Ivy that her mom said COVID times felt a little like the way she grew up in the 1970s. Kids stayed home, entertained themselves, and had way too much screen time.

"But 1970s kids could play together!" they both exclaimed in unison. They looked at each other and laughed, shaking their heads. It was so funny how in-sync they were.

"My mom always talked about how the slower pace of life in the beginning of COVID reminded her of her brief stint on the Greek island of Icaria and the whole healthy Mediterranean lifestyle that she loves so much," added Ivy.

Ivy liked hearing stories about her mom's time on the island, because her mom looked so happy when she told the stories. Her mom loved the sense of community and balance that was woven into their daily lives.

Ivy shared her mom's experiences of living with an Icarian family with Jayla. She explained that they would wake up early and work hard until mid-day. After a simple lunch, they would sometimes take a rest before going back to work for another couple of hours. Since they were generally done with work by 3:00 p.m., they'd have the whole afternoon to spend with friends and family or to develop hobbies.

"That sounds like how my parents spend vacation days!" remarked Jayla.

Ivy said, "It seems like a lot of Icarians have interesting hobbies and jobs that helped make stuff for the community. My mom said that they lived simply and didn't have all of the distractions that Americans do with running all over the place every day. The stories Ivy's mom shared didn't include much driving. Instead, most people walked and biked wherever they needed to go. They got their exercise by living an interesting and varied active life, rather than working out at gyms.

"My mom told me how she liked the evening meals that regularly doubled as potluck dinner parties. Everyone brought something and somehow it all worked out," added Ivy, "I guess the dining table always held a jug of homemade red wine or beer, and the entrees were typically plant based and came from someone's garden."

Then Ivy laughed and added, "My mom tried to emulate this rhythm in the States, but she always complained that Americans were too focused on themselves. It was impossible to implement a communal lifestyle alone."

Jayla said softly, "I miss the times when our families would hang out together all the time."

Ivy nodded as a big lump in her throat made it hard for her to swallow. They recognized that the community they once knew was a little fractured after Keith and Viola divorced. The two families used to take vacations together, and do movie nights, bike rides, and so many other fun outings together. After the divorce, it was awkward for Jayla's parents because they felt like they would be choosing sides if they saw either Keith or Viola.

Jayla said, "You know what? I think I may have read about that island in one of my dad's old *National Geographic* issues. I think Icaria was featured along with other "blue zones" where people experience incredible longevity." She paused for a moment as if searching her memory. "I think the point of the article was that people with such long lives tend to have a healthy diet, low stress, plenty of exercise through daily physical work, and close relationships. Why wouldn't everyone want to slow down and have a long and happy life like that?"

Jayla and Ivy sat in comfortable silence for a while with a boisterous cardinal singing in the background before Ivy broke the silence with a personal revelation.

"Jayla! Think about other times in history when a cultural revolution took place—like the end of slavery. When a child, regardless of gender or color, learns about slavery, he or she is automatically horrified. The system was, without question, morally bankrupt, inhumane, and absolutely mind-bogglingly wrong. No explanation could ever justify it. Americans resisted change for a long time, saying they knew slavery was wrong, but it was the basis of their economy, so it was too hard to change. That situation mirrors our modern dependence on fossil fuels to support the world economy, don't you think?"

"Wow. Yeah," replied Jayla.

Ivy continued, "Today, people know fossil fuels are killing people and that it's wrong, but they just throw up their hands and say, 'It's just too hard to change.'"

"Yep," agreed Jayla, "Not taking action is telling our generation and future generations that we aren't worth saving. How can people act like they love their kids so much and yet rip their futures away from them by not ensuring that they will have clean air to breathe in a livable climate?"

Ivy stated loudly, "Trillions of dollars are still being poured into COVID research, treatments, company bailouts, and relief money to individuals worldwide. If just billions of dollars were poured into tackling the climate crisis and people changed their lifestyles just a little to match the existential threat we are facing, we'd solve the problem."

Jayla jumped in with, "But, no. It's just clean up the latest disaster and then it's business as usual, completely ignoring the larger picture. It doesn't make any sense!" Shaking her head, Jayla continued, "How is it that two teenagers can plainly see a clear path forward, but world leaders can't?"

"Or won't," stated Ivy.

They decided that the lifestyle they both wanted to be a part of would be based on values rather than dictating specific actions. Essentially it was a life where people value money and possessions less, and time, health, and peace of mind more. As Ivy searched the web, she found that their idea and her mom's ideas of voluntary simplicity were not unique. There was even a term for the lifestyle: downshifting.

Compared to driving a manual car where a person shifts gears, "downshifting" referred to consciously trading a high-paying, but often stressful, career or lifestyle for one that was less pressured and perhaps less highly paid, but more fulfilling and balanced. It meant choosing to work toward simple living with fewer material things and adopting a more frugal and sustainable lifestyle with an improved quality of life so that a person had time for the important things in life, like friends and family. This lifestyle emphasized passion and purpose, meaning, fulfillment, and happiness.

"Essentially," summarized Jayla, "downshifting pretty much guarantees living a life without regrets."

They decided that they didn't really like the term "downshifting" because most kids their age didn't know anything about driving a manual car. They had to google the term to figure out what it was referring to. Plus, the word "down" connoted "less than" or "worse." This lifestyle wouldn't be worse. It would be better for people, relationships, the planet, and the future.

They decided that a better way to describe the lifestyle they imagined was summed up well by Mahatma Gandhi: "Live simply so others may simply live."

"A wasteful lifestyle takes resources away from other people, some of whom aren't even born yet," said Ivy.

"Yeah, the extravagant, consumptive lifestyle and driving enormous vehicles, is essentially stealing resources from others and the future," added Jayla. "Simplicity looks different for everyone, but it's always something to strive for."

"It reminds me of that quote from Paramahansa Yogananda that your mom has hanging in the entryway," Jayla said, "'Be as simple as you can be; you will be astonished to see how uncomplicated and happy your life can become.'"

Ivy nodded in agreement, and grabbed another slice of pizza, "That's kind of the essence of the new lifestyle we're promoting, isn't it?"

They sat again in silence, as the birds chattered away. After a while, Jayla reminisced, "Hey, remember in Mr. Mulcahy's class when we learned about how the country pulled together to ration and recycle during World War II?"

"Sort of," replied Ivy, "I had a hard time paying attention in Mr. Mulcahy's class, honestly. I couldn't ever pay attention to anything except for his toupee. I was sure that if I watched it long enough I'd see it fall off."

Jayla laughed and agreed, "It was kind of absurd that his toupee sat on the top of his head and there was an inch of space between it and his hairline, wasn't it?"

Ivy said, "I wish I would've paid a little more attention, I guess, because everyone needs to be a part of the war on climate change in the same way, and rethink our relationships with what we purchase and eat."

Jayla said, "Hashtag Live Simply."

Ivy added, "Hashtag It's Not All About You."

Jayla laughed and added "We're All In this Together."

Ivy replied, "That sounds so COVID. How about, hashtag Victory Life?"

CHAPTER 10

You Got Ejected?

Viola was feeling serene as she drove back from her yoga workshop. Well, at least until Keith appeared from no where in the passenger seat next to her. She screamed and nearly swerved off the road at the sight of him as she hollered, "Jeee-sus H. Schnickelfritz Haufen Mist Christ! Where in the HELL did you come from?"

Keith had to chuckle about Viola's swearing. Even Germans didn't use the Schnitzelbank song lyrics as swear words. Keith found it rather endearing, but judging from the look on Viola's face, he realized she only wanted answers.

He quickly answered, "I was ejected from the planet, and I need your help."

"Wait," Viola questioned ignoring the whole ejected part, "You're supposed to be with Ivy this weekend. Who's with Ivy?"

Keith replied, "Um, yeah, it's not like I chose to get ejected from the planet, Vi. I checked in with her. She's a smart girl. She's OK. She's helping me." He went on to summarize the events of the past day.

Viola replied, "So, let me get this straight. You didn't pick up Ivy last night because you got *ejected* from the planet?" Viola asked her ex-husband incredulously. "And you were somewhere in the mesosphere, with a bunch of other people, who were also ejected from Earth because they shared in the responsibility for our planetary ills," she added flatly.

"Yes, that's what happened to me," said Keith.

"You got ejected from the world," she repeated slowly enunciating every word. "You were in space and met people from all over the world. And then you went on a scary, apocalyptic tour, and now you can't get back to Earth unless you convince people to cut their carbon footprints in half?"

"Umm, yes, that about sums it up," agreed Keith.

Viola had fallen out of love with her ex, but she had never pegged him as delusional. Since she had been at the yoga retreat, she hadn't heard any news, so she didn't know anything about what he was telling her. She was beginning to question her own sanity as she spoke to a glowing, angelic version of her ex-husband.

"So, if you're from a different world, or whatever, how can I talk to you now?" asked Viola.

"I turned my voice setting on," Keith replied, "I didn't have that setting figured out when I communicated with Ivy. She couldn't hear me or see me, so we communicated through Morse code."

"Ivy knows Morse code?" questioned Viola.

"YouTube," answered Keith.

Viola's puzzlement turned into an ah-that-makes-sense kind of nod.

Keith continued, "I just slipped a large carbon tax into the national energy bill and…"

Viola interrupted, "What? A carbon tax? You? How? You sold your soul to the devil years ago, remember?"

"Yes, I do," said Keith with downcast eyes.

"So, you admit it?" asked Viola.

"Yeah, I lost my way, Viola. I lost my moral compass," answered Keith without hesitating.

"I never thought I'd hear you say that." Viola's demeanor softened and she wanted to know more. "So, you just slipped in a carbon tax? Just like that. Single-handedly. I've been working on that for decades," Viola said doubtfully.

Keith couldn't tell if that last part of the comment was incredulousness or jealousy, but he explained, "There are some advantages to being in the world I'm in right now. I'm finding that anything is possible. I was able to change the final emergency energy bill before the president signed it this morning," explained Keith, "After that bill was signed into law, I thought about how I needed a champion to implement these taxes and, of course, I thought of you. Then, as I floated up in the troposphere, I saw a bright light in this area, and I was drawn to it. I couldn't help but move toward the light. As it turns out, I was drawn straight to you."

Viola responded impatiently, "Troposphere now? Before you were way up in the mesosphere."

"Look, I know how crazy this sounds. But yeah, it's a big universe out there, and I kind of guess where I'm at based on how much of the Earth I can see," Keith replied quickly.

"So, let me get this straight, you went toward 'the light,' and you were drawn to me. It sounds like an end-of-life scenario to me," Viola said flatly, "Are we both dead?" she asked as she started making weird noises and slapping herself.

Keith had to laugh. Why was this the go-to response when people questioned their vitality? Keith assured her that she was still very much alive, saying, "I think you are the link to putting these taxes into effect, Viola. Wasn't that always the plan?"

Viola's jaw dropped as tears involuntarily streamed down her face. *Could it be, her ex wasn't morally bankrupt after all?*

"I need someone to use the carbon tax revenue to invest in clean energy infrastructure, passive building design, and the retrofitting of existing buildings to make them energy efficient. You are the person to lead this revolution, Viola," explained Keith.

She smiled and, nodding through her tears, accepted the position without hesitation.

Leave it to Viola to not look back or hold a grudge, thought Keith. She truly was made of superior stock. Full of grace, forgiveness, strength, and intelligence. At that very moment, it struck him that this is what love looks like.

Viola felt overwhelmed, yet energized at the task of revolutionizing the energy world. Where would she start? Despite such a massive task laying ahead of her she felt amazingly light, content, decisive, and confident. She recognized that she had been waiting for this moment her whole life. As she looked at Keith, her spirits lifted. She felt alive for the first time in years. She started to laugh. Once she started to laugh, she couldn't stop. It became a channel to release all of the intensity of the situation: the surprise and the initial fear of Keith popping into her car, his sudden about-face on climate change, and the feeling of connecting with life partner and her life's purpose all rolled into one.

She pulled off the road to finish laughing and they shared a long embrace and kiss. And then he disappeared as quickly as he had appeared. She wished he would've stayed longer, but it was a gift to have him back to his true self again. She recalled how often she and Keith used to laugh together and how she would periodically fall off stools from laughing so hard with him. She realized that Keith truly was her soulmate and that she would always love him.

CHAPTER 11

Voilà

When Viola got home, she greeted Ivy and Jayla with big hugs. Ivy and Viola exchanged stories about their unbelievable encounters with Keith, and they discussed the inconceivable situation they were in the middle of. Ivy and Jayla outlined their plan, and Viola agreed it sounded good. Viola shared that she was also planning to start with energy efficiency and passive housing in low-income areas.

Viola took back her office from Ivy. After she got settled, she dove into reading the new 499 page national energy policy. It was genius. It included everything that she had hoped it would. And it really helped that the climate crisis had been declared a national emergency to unite the country's actions.

She knew that the most vulnerable communities were her priority, and she wanted to lift up the low-income neighborhoods that had been purposefully mistreated and "redlined" by city planners in the mid-1950s. Redlining was a practice used around the country to disrupt, even annihilate communities of color. In Minnesota, Interstate 94 was built right through the heart of the thriving, predominantly black Rondo Neighborhood. Hundreds of people and businesses were forced to evacuate and one in every eight African Americans in St. Paul lost a home to I-94. Many of those businesses never reopened.[29]

On top of redlining, it was common to have covenants for houses that read: "Premises shall not be sold, mortgaged, or leased to or occupied by any person or persons other than members of the Caucasian race."[30]

So, where were people supposed to go? thought Viola. These covenants were a part of systematic segregation that created wealth for white people and poverty for non-whites. Since one of the best ways to accumulate wealth was to invest in a house, families that could buy houses in nice neighborhoods saw their home values soar and could then pass that wealth onto the next generation. Families that couldn't buy homes simply did not have the opportunity to build wealth for their children to inherit.[31]

The thing that drove Viola crazy about this horribly racist situation was that an alternative was suggested by a St. Paul city engineer named George Harrold. He opposed going right through the Rondo Neighborhood, citing concerns about loss of land for local use and the dislocation of people and business. But, in the end, government officials approved the original route, citing its efficiency. *Now, don't tell me this would have been the most "efficient" route if this had not been a Black neighborhood,* thought Viola angrily.

Across the nation, as if these neighborhoods weren't subjected to enough abuse, low-income neighborhoods were also often treated like dumps where the polluting factories were put. They had the worst air quality and the most health issues associated with the poor air quality, like asthma and heart disease. *They seriously can't breathe,* thought Viola as she saw the irony between George Floyd's dying words and the larger situation. It was no accident that the worst polluters were placed in and near these mostly black and brown neighborhoods.

Viola met some of the people in her gardening club who were interviewed for a documentary about the Rondo Neighborhood. They had fascinating stories that all echoed how the neighborhood was described as almost utopian, where everybody knew everybody and how there were businesses and medical facilities of every kind. Neighborhood schools provided educations, and the community took care of each other. Everything a person needed to grow up and become a productive adult was right there. And then whites destroyed it. It made her cry.

Yes, a good place to start to move the needle on climate change would be with efficient heating and cooling in low-income neighborhoods. *Since heating and cooling houses makes up about seventeen percent of a person's carbon footprint, let's start there and bring that way down, maybe even to zero.* She knew her obsession with passive houses informed Ivy's plan. She was proud that some of her teaching and preaching had rubbed off on her daughter and Jayla, too, her second daughter.

The clear answer was getting passive houses to be the norm. Passive houses are so energy efficient, with two-foot thick walls and triple-glazed windows, they don't even need heating or cooling systems. Even though there were more building materials needed for the construction of these houses due to the thick walls and more expensive windows, not needing expensive heating or cooling systems largely offset the added expenses. Plus, the houses no longer had energy bills, so they paid for themselves in a matter of years.

Viola's nonprofit became instrumental in creating a national passive home upgrade program with carbon tax dollars that funded retrofitting structurally sound houses and rebuilding dilapidated ones. The result was neighborhoods of modern houses that had sleek, bright, cozy interiors. This program created a lot of well-paid jobs for architects, engineers, builders, developers, carpenters, electricians, and plumbers.

When communities couldn't find enough paid trade labor, they came together for "house raising" parties that were reminiscent of the eighteenth- and nineteenth-century "barn raising" parties. These were joyful events, filled with great food and music. Since the passive houses were twice as energy efficient, even without other drastic energy reductions, the rest of the home energy use was relatively easy to provide with renewables. Solar panels were placed on roofs wherever possible, which then supplied the rest of their energy needs—they even charged people's electric cars. When rooftop solar wasn't feasible, she made sure their energy was coming from a wind or solar farm. Thirty-two percent of home emissions can be virtually eliminated. Voilà!

Of course, reducing energy use within the household, shouldn't be completely ignored, thought Viola. Water heaters and clothes dryers were a big energy suck, with a combined twenty-one percent of the home energy use total. *How will this be tackled,* Viola wondered?

CHAPTER 12

Toward Depolarization

Reports about the Ejected dominated the news all around the world. To bring approximately five percent of the world's population—and nearly twenty-five percent of the U.S. population—back to Earth, the world would have to work together to significantly reduce their footprints.

About eighty percent of the U.S. population felt obliged to do their part to bring down the CO_2e, because they were either personally separated from a loved one or knew someone who was. These people became known as the "Collectivists," and they generally believed it was common sense to help reunite loved ones, save lives, and give children a future.

In general, Collectivists didn't find it hard to adopt the "Victory Life" since new smart grid technologies and renewables allowed people to maintain their comfortable lifestyles with a fraction of the previous CO_2e footprint. To boot, a saner pace of life that allowed for more time to be spent with loved ones was widely welcomed. Suddenly, the idea of "working to live"—a comfortable, but not extravagant, lifestyle—was much more popular and socially acceptable than the old "living to work"—and basically not having time to do anything else but work to support expensive lifestyles. As a whole, Collectivists viewed the changes in society positively and found their lives to be happier when they were more connected with people rather than with their possessions.

The other roughly twenty percent of U.S. society, who didn't acknowledge climate change as being a threat, became known as "Independents." The Independents generally didn't see it as their responsibility to care for vulnerable people or to help people they didn't know. Their focus was primarily on preserving their own freedoms.

Although the Collectivists struggled with why the Independents didn't seem to be concerned with other people's freedoms and Independents didn't understand why Collectivists were supporting tax increases, both sides began to recognize that using "us" and "them" language, name-calling, and broad stereotypes didn't do any good. It certainly didn't change minds. It just tore friends and family apart. There was a concerted effort to depolarize the country by respecting and appreciating differences of opinions. It was no longer acceptable to express hatred, disdain, or pity toward people with opposing views. Emphasis was placed on civility, respect, and finding common ground.

But what really pulled the U.S. together was the realization that if society continued using so many fossil fuels, they could potentially lose their freedoms. After all, without a livable climate, there is no health, well-being, or future. Although it might seem obvious that there are no freedoms for people to enjoy if humanity gets wiped out, putting the situation into these terms was an "ah-ha!" moment for many Americans. Preserving the country's freedoms seemed to be something that people on both sides could get behind.

Gone would be the land of opportunity, regardless of social class. Gone would be the country known for rewarding hard-working citizens with prosperity and success. The American Dream, founded upon equality, life, liberty, and the pursuit of happiness, simply wouldn't be possible for future generations if current behaviors and attitudes didn't change quickly. How would anyone be able to pursue these inalienable rights if they were suffering from an unlivable climate, dirty air and water, and contaminated soils? Environmental conservation soon became synonymous with patriotism.

✳✳✳

Pat was a server at the local diner who identified with the Independents. She had raised four kids on her own and was a do-it-herself-er through and through—out of necessity at first and preference later on. She learned that she was the most reliable person she knew. Her entire life she'd had to rely on herself, so it felt natural for her to side with the Independents.

One of Pat's many skills was serving the entire diner without writing a single order down. It took four cooks to keep up with her orders. Sometimes, when the cooks got behind, she'd run back to the line and cook the food herself. She was so good at her job that she could usually guess what a person was going to order just by looking at him or her, even if the person wasn't a regular. She had an uncanny ability to size up the morning coffee drinkers versus the Diet Coke drinkers. Sure, she was a little prickly with her customers at times, and didn't suffer fools lightly—or anyone who hesitated, or asked too many questions either. But that was what kept people coming back. She called the shots with blunt honesty, yet still remained very likable.

Besides her kids and grandkids, what she loved most was her 1957 Cadillac DeVille. It was the most beautiful car in the county—maybe even the state. Every time she took it out for a spin, she felt like the Queen of Sheba. All eyes were on her. She feared that the carbon tax that the Collectivists supported would push her hobby out of her price range. She certainly didn't trust the politicians who stated that working class people, like her, wouldn't feel higher prices. In her mind, it made sense for her to protect her lifestyle and she saw it as her God-given right to carry on as she wanted.

What made Pat reconsider her views was a conversation she had with her 15-year-old granddaughter Jill.

"I don't care about goin' to school, Grandma," stated Jill when her grandma questioned why she was at the diner during school hours, "The climate's gonna be too hot by the time I'm grown up. It'll probably be unlivable by the time I'm forty. So, what's the point? I'm just going to enjoy my life. And I don't enjoy school."

Her granddaughter's passing comment stopped Pat in her tracks. *Did Jill really believe this?* Pat spun on her heal, stared at Jill for a long moment, and plunked herself down into a booth. She'd never thought of the future in those bleak terms before. And if there was one regret she'd had, it was dropping out of high school to marry Hank. She made up her mind in an instant.

"Well, Jill. You're gonna have a bright future. I don't agree with everything the Collectivists are doing, but they're right about taking care of the next generation. Now, you go back to school. You're clever. You have lots of options. Don't get stuck waiting tables your whole life like me. My body's giving out. And what will I do when I can't work anymore?"

Pat had been hearing the buzz about depolarization, but hadn't paid attention until that moment. She decided she would stop name-calling and stereotyping and start listening, acknowledging other points of view, and work towards mutual respect. The kids deserved that. The hatred and pettiness had to stop on both sides for the sake of humanity.

Soon Pat found out that even Collectivists could appreciate a really cool old car. And some of them weren't too stuck-up either. She also came to realize that society worked better when everyone was cared for. She loosened her grip on needing to be so independent and found that she enjoyed weaving her life into the community so she could support others—and *be* supported by others.

Little by little, progress was made to get people to see each other as people, not as stereotypes. Pat realized that people can differ widely on policies and ideas like what role the government should have, and still have similar ultimate goals for the country and its people. In the end, she decided that neither side is going to completely overcome the other, so we better figure out how to get along and run the country together.

MISSION POSSIBLES:

A Collection of Stories from other Ejecteds

CHAPTER 13

The Cost of Hot Water

A lifetime of excessive hot water use landed Heather with the Ejected. "But did you ever really have a chance?" her Defender teased her. "Your name is Heather or 'heat' plus 'her.' Just take out the second "h" and you get 'heater,' as in hot water heater." Heather was not amused by her Defender's sense of humor.

Hot water was, perhaps, subconsciously a part of her identity, Heather silently acknowledged. She took long showers, sometimes several times a day. She ran her dishwasher every evening, whether it was full or not, and did excessive amounts of laundry in hot water. But her biggest water use was her baths with the water all the way to the top. For most U.S. residents, hot water makes up about thirteen percent of their energy use,[32] but as Heather learned on her tour, it was around fifty percent for her.

Those long baths were a ritual and luxury that Heather clung to. Each night after her kids went to bed, she would draw herself a bath and let the water run continuously so it didn't get cold. She had two little kids who never freakin' slept through the night, and she felt entitled to a little pampering. The little one had asthma like her, and she never knew if she was going to be up at night doing nebulizer treatments with him. She never set out to be a single parent, but that was how life turned out for her ever since her husband, Jason, had been accidentally shot and killed by his best friend, Donovan. The same Donovan who had introduced Heather and Jason—and just happened to be Heather's older brother.

Jason and Donovan started hanging out in college, where they met at the University of Minnesota. They were placed together at the Comstock dorm freshmen year and chose to live with each other for the rest of college. During their junior year, Jason got scheduled to work over the long Thanksgiving weekend, so he didn't have time for the twelve-hour-round-trip drive to and from Chicago. Since he was stuck in Minneapolis for the weekend and couldn't be with his own family, Donovan invited him to his grandparents' house. Jason met thirty-six relatives of Donovan's—including his sister, Heather. Jason and Heather were an instant match and dated for a couple of years until she also finished college. They settled down in Golden Valley, a first-ring Minneapolis suburb, and welcomed "Irish twin" boys, who were 11 months apart, into their family shortly after they married.

When Heather and Jason's boys were three and four, Jason, her brother, and five other college friends took their annual guys' weekend to Heather and Donovan's family's cabin. They tended to drink too much on these weekends, but it was generally tame. However, this particular weekend, things got out of hand. Donovan showed off an old gun when he did the unthinkable. He pulled the trigger as a joke, thinking the safety was on. Instead of a stupid joke, he shot and killed his best friend, his sister's husband, and the father of his nephews.

Heather tried not to hate her brother for what he had done, because she knew that it was an accident and that he suffered, too. But her pain and resentment ran deep. *How could my brother be so stupid?* she would ruminate often. Her true love and her children's daddy was snatched away because of Donovan's stupidity. Growing up, Heather and Donovan's dad always taught them gun safety and not to point a gun at anything or anyone unless they intended to kill it. But her brother was so thick-skulled that he wouldn't even learn that simple lesson. His stupidity shattered her life.

So, Heather felt entitled to that hot water to help soothe her pain. She never thought twice about her hot water usage or considered hot water to have any sort of an environmental impact. Even if someone would have explained the impact, she wasn't sure that she would have cared. It wasn't like she was an uncaring person; she was trying to survive and heal her own personal trauma.

Heather wasn't much different than the other Midwesterners who took hot water for granted. Even when the temperature dropped to -30 °F outside, everyone expected instant hot water from their taps.

The first part of Heather's tour was visiting several "asthma capital" cities with poor air quality around the U.S. Her Defender exacerbated her chronic asthma and then made enormous sewer rats chase her up and down the streets to make her feel the effects of poor air quality caused by the nearby coal-burning power plants. As she huffed, panted, and fought for each breath, she cursed the smoggy air and realized that her actions did negatively impact others, even if she couldn't see the effect and never intended it.

Heather learned that water heaters typically used natural gas or electricity generated from coal-burning power plants. Both of those energy sources had negative impacts on water and greenhouse gas emissions. Even though natural gas burned cleaner than oil and coal, emissions alone did not tell the full story. Heather learned that the drilling and extraction of natural gas from wells and its transportation in pipelines ended up leaking methane—the primary component of natural gas that was eighty-six times stronger than carbon dioxide at trapping heat over a twenty-year period.[33]

Heather saw communities whose drinking water, groundwater, and lakes and rivers were contaminated with hazardous fracking chemicals. She witnessed improperly managed chemicals that spilled out of faulty storage containers or leaked during transport. She also saw communities that lacked residential water supplies because the groundwater was used in the fracking process. She conceded to her

Defender that natural gas wasn't a great solution for hot water heaters, so her Defender took her to experience electric water heaters that came from popular coal-burning power plants.

To make Heather understand the amount of water used in coal-burning power plants, Heather was dropped at the bottom of Niagara Falls. The water violently crashed her around, and she felt like a sock in a washing machine. It was the scariest event of her life. She thought she was about to drown when the Defender plucked her out from beneath one of the world's largest waterfalls and heaved her onto the observatory deck. Limp and unable to move, Heather listened to the Defender explain that every single minute the U.S. used three times the amount of water she experienced flowing over Niagara Falls in a minute to generate electricity through coal and nuclear energy.[34]

Heather's Defender explained, "Another way to look at this is that with coal and nuclear, more water is generally required to generate the electricity that lights our rooms, powers our computers, and runs our appliances than the total amount of water we use in our homes for everyday tasks like washing, showering, flushing, and watering lawns and gardens."[35]

Not only did creating hot water heated with natural gas and coal have a horrible carbon footprint, but it also had a horrible water footprint. It took massive amounts of water to create steam and cool the equipment. It was clearly a bad deal, and now that she knew about the situation and the urgency of climate change, she realized that society's reaction didn't match reality. The clear takeaways from Heather's mission were that people should use less hot water in general, and hot water heaters should be powered by renewable energy.

Heather missed her kids so much that she could barely function. She felt like part of her was missing. They were little extensions of her and Jason, and they were part of what kept Jason alive for Heather. She'd do anything to kiss her kids and have her lips sink into her boys' smooth, squishy cheeks. She missed hearing the squeals of joy that would follow those kisses. She had to get back to her boys. She didn't care if she'd ever get a warm bath again if she could just get a warm hug from her boys—the cuddliest little monsters ever.

Thankfully, there already was a team of Ejected working on switching hot water heating to solar, so her mission was focused on behaviors and habits. At first, she considered zeroing in on dishwashers, but after she learned that they removed about four hundred times the bacteria than washing dishes by hand,[36] she decided to leave that alone. Instead, she decided to focus on setting people's washing machines to cold and delivering efficient showerheads and shower timers to people not already using those devices. Doing the washing machines was super easy. She'd just switch the settings to cold, and no one even realized it.

Changing people's showering habits was a more complicated task. For the stubborn people who didn't install the low-flow showerheads, she had to resort to coming in and shutting people's water off. She'd watch the clock, and when their allotted five-minute showers were up, Heather would shut the water off. You'd think that she would just turn the hot water off, but Heather had a mean streak. Instead, she turned off the water supply to the home completely so people were forced to remain soapy. *I love working people into a lather,* she'd think, and then she'd laugh at her own stupid joke.

Most people learned to change their behaviors and started taking shorter, cooler showers—or at least using less soap. However, there were some stupid people she encountered who never learned. They just strolled about, a bit baffled that no one else walked around with dried soap caked onto themselves.

CHAPTER 14

Just Say No

Nancy Wagon ended up with the Ejected for her excessive energy use and promotion of clothes dryers. In the 1980s, First Lady Nancy Reagan's War on Drugs ad campaign slogan "Just Say No" took on a different meaning when Nancy Wagon adopted the familiar slogan for her anti-clothesline campaign. She was out to rid the world of ugly and embarrassing clotheslines. "Are we *peasants* who need to hang-dry our clothes because we can't afford a civilized way of drying them?" she'd ask.

She was a leader in the condo and townhouse association world and had connections. She gave passionate talks at conferences and bought airtime on local cable stations, ranting about the insidiousness of clotheslines. She would look straight into the camera and ask, "What self-respecting person would ever hang their laundry—especially their *undergarments*—out in the open for the world to see? Clotheslines are old-fashioned, uncivilized, and discourteous gadgets that need to be banned. If you put one up, the next neighbor will put one up, too. On and on it will spread like a virus, and soon respectable towns will look like shantytowns," she'd warn. Nancy Wagon considered clotheslines a lower-class symbol.

For years to come, and at every chance she got, Ms. Wagon touted her accomplishment of successfully banning clotheslines from nearly every condo and townhouse association in the nation. No matter what the social setting, from picnics and cocktail parties, to receiving communion from her priest and brief interactions with Girl Scouts selling cookies, Nancy Wagon could skillfully voice her disdain of clotheslines in any situation. Being around Nancy was as much of a boring and painful experience as it was joyless. She could talk of nothing else other than herself and her obsessive hatred for clotheslines.

As it turns out, Nancy didn't really need to be so neurotic. Her anti-clothesline platform was already becoming the norm because society gravitated toward adopting the path of least resistance. It was faster to throw clothes in a dryer. As a result, clotheslines became virtually extinct in the western hemisphere, with ninety-two percent of U.S. homes and eighty-one percent of Canadian homes using only dryers.[37] Whereas, the rest of the world never fully adopted clothes dryers and seemed to get along just fine.

Now Nancy was charged with undoing her life's work because hang-drying clothes would lead to closing forty-two coal-fired energy plants and reduce the average U.S. homeowner's energy bill by seven to eight percent.[38] But what really shook Nancy on her tour was the fact that if America did hang-dry laundry, they could save lives. Particulate emissions from burning coal led to air pollution that caused about 222 deaths each day.[39] Her niece died from asthma, so this statistic hit close to home. On top of those deaths, thirteen people died each year because of dryer fires.[40] To put these numbers in other terms, the impact of dryers accounted for triple the number of deaths caused by terrorism each year in the U.S.[41] Shocking. Clotheslines *saved* lives. Imagine that.

CHAPTER 15

Flipping Farming

A large number of the Ejected were in the "eating" fewer greenhouse gases group. Since there were so many issues related to the food footprint, the Ejected decided to divide the tasks into workgroups and sub-work groups.

1. Encouraging 'flipped farming' (no-till/low-till methods to lock the carbon into the soil instead of releasing it through tilling)
2. Maximizing food efficiency (minimize food waste, packaging, miles)
3. Making cookstoves and ovens (especially in developing countries) more sustainable

Doris was the leader of the "farm flipping" group. By "farm flipping," the Ejected weren't referring to buying farms, fixing them up, and reselling them for a quick profit like flipping houses, but rather turning agriculture on its head by changing a basic farming practice. That practice was to stop—or at least minimize—tilling the fields.

On the Ejected tour, Doris' group learned that plowing releases gigatons of carbon dioxide into the atmosphere[42] and that world agriculture/land use contributes twenty-four percent of the global greenhouse gas emissions.[43] Who knew? She was raised to think that plowing was essential to break up the fields to turn organic matter into soil. She thought it was done to help add nutrients to the soil by having the oxygen help speed up the decomposition of the leftover plant matter from the previous season.

As a group, the farmers felt defensive about being culpable for climate change. From their point of view, farmers were the good guys just trying to feed people. Farmers weren't in the business for fame and fortune, after all. They were helping the community by providing food. In addition, farming was a tough business because their boss was Mother Nature, and she could be as relentless, unforgiving, unfair, moody, and unpredictable as she was glorious. All of these farmers had worked their whole lives as farmers—many of their families had been in the business for generations—toiling away to feed the nation. Conventional farming was the just way everyone farmed.

As dedicated farmers, they all knew that healthy soils were, literally, the foundation of healthy ecosystems and bountiful crops. On their tour, they watched two farming scenarios unfold side by side with the conventional farming routine that they were accustomed to progress on the left and no-till agriculture on the right. The difference not tilling made to reduce emissions, as well as a whole host of other positive benefits, was astonishing.

As Doris watched the side-by-side comparison, she had a silly thought. The circular nature of farming reminded her of a children's book her kids had adored called *If You Give a Mouse a Cookie*. This book also had a circular format. She had read it so often she could practically recite it word for word even now, decades later. In this cute book, the mouse received a cookie and an unexpected sequence occurred. In the end, that mouse ended up exactly where he started, wanting another cookie.

The two different farming scenarios unfolded two very different sequences, and Doris amused herself by imagining how each scenario could be made into a sad version or a happy version of the book. The sad version that would retell what was actually happening across the nation and would surely leave the kids despondent. On the other hand, the happy version would tell the story of regenerative agriculture that would end with the world in a better place, alive with delightful butterflies and beautiful rainbows.

So, instead of giving a mouse a cookie, thought Doris as if she were rewriting the book using traditional farming methods, *it might read something like this: When we give a farmer a plow, the plowing releases enormous amounts of carbon dioxide into the atmosphere. Since plowing destroys the pore spaces in the soil, the microbes that keep the soil healthy and that depend on those pore spaces die.*

She imagined how sad it would be to have to tell a group of kids, *'Let's say goodbye to the microbes, kids!'*

'And without those lovely pore spaces,' she would explain to an imaginary class of lower elementary school kids seated on a reading rug, *'the water cannot infiltrate into the soil, so the precious prairie soils get washed away. Can you say <u>erosion</u>?'*

'And, oh dear! What happens next, children? The soil washes into nearby creeks and chokes the fish!' This would surely prompt a kid to make dramatic choking noises as if he were one of those poor fish.

She walked across her field and noticed the gully washes where the rain made valleys in her fields. *So, if we wouldn't have plowed, most of the water would have been able to soak into the ground.*

She remembered reading in a farm journal that erosion was more of a problem today than it was in the dust bowl of the 1930's. But somehow, no one spoke about it. *Why is that?* she wondered, *Is it because there are just too many crises for people these days? Our most valuable natural resource here in Iowa is our rich soil made from layers of prairie plants that formed over millennia and it is getting flushed away in a matter of decades.*

And here's where plowing gets expensive, thought Doris. *This erosion leads to a loss of nutrients, and loss of nutrients leads to needing to add synthetic fertilizers. These fertilizers are so expensive, and those chemical fertilizers add a lot of nitrogen—a nutrient which most weeds love. So, let's all spend more money we don't have to buy herbicides to kill those weeds*, she thought sardonically.

Since herbicides bind to micronutrient metals—like magnesium, manganese, iron, zinc, and copper—they are unavailable to the plants. "Good thing we spent all that money on fertilizer," Doris found herself saying aloud.

She gazed at her beautiful field, and it hurt her to realize that she had unknowingly caused harm to the land she loved. A single tear rolled down her cheek. She continued reflecting upon what she had learned on the tour. *If the plants cannot take up these micronutrients, they are more prone to disease. These weaker plants cannot ward off diseases on their own, so they may need to be sprayed with fungicides, which are also detrimental to the microbes in the soil. These weakened plants may also not be able to ward off pests, so then in come the pesticides too.*

Here's where Doris envisioned farmers across the world hitting their palms to their foreheads as they uttered a loud, Homer Simpson-like, "Doh!"

The pesticides kill predator insects, which likely would have otherwise taken care of the pest insects we are trying to control. 'But sadly, children, now we have also decimated the good bugs like the pollinators,' she thought resuming her imaginary cautionary tale. *We need to keep growing food, so we start the process of wasting money and harming the environment all over again with more plowing.*

On her tour, Doris and the other farmers learned there was a flip side—an alternative way to farm that didn't set off this unfortunate chain of events. It all started with <u>not</u> plowing. She envisioned herself and her husband in hammocks sipping ice tea while her neighbors toiled away with early spring, plowing the second the fields were dry enough to plow. Oh, the scorn and the gossip that would ensue. *'Did you see that Doris and Harvey didn't plow their fields?'* she imagined the conversation starting. *'Are they OK?'* someone might ask. *'Oh, yeah. So-and-so spotted them lazing in their hammocks all day sipping ice-cold beverages.'*

To be lazy in the farming world was a cardinal sin. A farmer could be a lot of negative qualities and still be respected—ornery, uneducated, stubborn, chauvinistic, or disagreeable were nothing in comparison to laziness.

On their tour, they had learned that practicing regenerative soil techniques mimics natural processes and creates a narrative they'd like to be a part of. She found herself setting up the regenerative farming tale in the same Give-A-Mouse-A-Cookie-circular-format pretending to tell it to another classroom of kids.

'Now, children, if we don't start with plowing, keep the soil covered with cover crops, and disturb the soil as little as possible, we don't release the carbon stored in the soil.' The picture would be of soil sleeping with a big "do not disturb" sign on it. *'See? Do not disturb. And that's a very good thing, because that invisible gas belongs in the soil, not in the atmosphere.'* She realized going into the effects of greenhouse gases might be a little advanced for her audience, but she continued anyhow.

'See what happens next, boys and girls? The soil stays in place! It is not blown away by the wind or washed away by the rain. And you know what else happens?' she asked her fictional, highly-engaged class. *'We save water because we don't need to irrigate as often because it doesn't evaporate.'*

'And look at how lovely this scene is, kids!' she continued, *'Without soil erosion, we keep the nutrients in the soil where we want them. This saves farmers lots of money because they do not need to buy expensive fertilizers,'* she continued.

She flipped to the next page in her mind and cheerfully exclaimed, *'Look at how limiting erosion helps keep nearby lakes and rivers clean! And, boys and girls, without those synthetic fertilizers, we have more plant diversity—not just the weedy, nitrogen-loving species,'* she explained to her beloved imaginary students, who were such great listeners and hung on her every word without ever interrupting her.

Again, she realized that this vocabulary might be a bit complex, but she was amusing herself, so she kept on. *'And plant diversity means maintaining those critical pore spaces and building up rich organic matter in the soil. That organic matter nourishes the plants, so they are healthy and are better able to fight off disease and pests without the need for fungicides and pesticides. Cha-Ching! More money in Farmer Mom and Dad's pockets. And we can keep our beneficial pollinators—like butterflies and bees.'*

✷✷✷

The farmers discussed various solutions to implement no-till and conservation farming, as well as nutrient management—including biochar production. Biochar was a new idea to a lot of the farmers, but they learned that it is an ancient practice of baking organic materials without oxygen, so that gas and oil separate out resulting in fuels that can be used for energy and biochar that can be used to enrich soil.

They collectively decided that education was too slow. Everyone agreed people in general are creatures of habit and rooted in tradition. Besides, the consensus was that facts don't change enough peoples' minds these days. The idea that rose to the surface was making the carbon dioxide gas visible with an awful odor so people would be motivated to keep the CO_2 in the ground by not tilling so they wouldn't have to endure the stench.

Defender Seth really liked this idea of making the carbon dioxide stink. He suggested all kinds of putrid odors: rotten eggs, animal puke, a bloated dead whale, or how about a Stinking Corpse Lily that actually smells like a rotting corpse? Dead fish and sweaty socks were other popular options that were discussed. Defender Sam jumped in on the conversation and explained that research showed species have evolved to be grossed out by smells that could potentially harm them. It is a survival mechanism that people's brains respond differently to different smells.[44]

The course of history may be forever altered by this little bit of knowledge, coupled with people's biological aversion to bad smells.

The Defenders helped the Ejected design the CO_2 to smell repulsive to whomever was tilling, so they'd be forced to stop. People identified the smell of the carbon dioxide differently, but it was unanimously agreed that the smell was unbearable. It didn't take long for people around the world to adopt regenerative agriculture practices because they couldn't stand not to stop.

CHAPTER 16

"Eating" Fewer Emissions

Nina, Ayesha, and Nevaeh were all notoriously picky eaters who bonded during their Ejected tour. They were horrified to realize that years of over serving themselves and throwing away plates of food virtually untouched greatly contributed to the climate crisis. They had no idea that roughly one-third of the world's food is never eaten and is responsible for about eight percent of global emissions.[45] To make matters worse, they were saddened by the fact that not only was that food just going to waste while people were still starving; wasting food squandered other resources, like water, energy, and fertilizer.

"Think of the unnecessary deforestation for additional farmland that is creating gigatons of additional emissions," stated Ayesha in deep remorse. "These forests are needed to sequester the carbon dioxide and support countless plants and animals. Food waste generates greenhouse gases at every stage that are one hundred percent unnecessary."

Nevaeh chimed in with, "And if all of this weren't bad enough, when the food decomposes, hazardous methane is released."

Nina nodded along. This trio's goal in transforming food waste was to reduce emissions by about ninety gigatons[46] and she was put in charge of leading the group of Ejected that was tackling the food waste in high-income countries. This food waste problem was mainly caused by consumers' inattention to what was going bad in their fridges. Americans throw out an obscene $165 billion worth of food every year.[47] Why did people consistently waste their hard-earned money? This group of Ejected was puzzled about how to solve the problem because it was illogical. People worked really hard to buy this fresh produce, but they never got around to actually using it, and it rotted in their refrigerators. On top of the wasted food, it was typically stored in energy-demanding refrigerators. In short, people were accustomed to driving to the store, buying food, paying to store it, and never eating it.

To manage the home food wasters, Nina's group took a two-pronged approach. First, they would reduce over-sized portions by taking food off of peoples' plates. Most people didn't seem to notice. Next, they looked in refrigerators and put reminders on people's phones to check their refrigerators for food about to expire. Then they pushed recipes to them on their smartphones with ideas on how to use those foods as ingredients. The funny thing was people never questioned how or why they received these notifications. They just thought it was serendipity and didn't give it another thought.

For the people without smartphones, the Ejected just kept setting the food that was about to expire out on the counter, so it was visible. Most of the time, the visible cue was enough to make people act and use up the food. Sometimes, the people who encountered the food on the counter for the umpteenth time would holler at their spouses or kids for leaving food out. For her own amusement, Nina started messing with these people and started leaving other things out just to see their reactions.

Ayesha headed up the group of Ejected that worked in developing countries where food waste was an unintended consequence of inadequate infrastructure for storage, processing, and transportation. Ayesha's supply chain and engineering skills came in handy, and her creativity, coupled with communication skills, made her perfectly suited to carry out the tasks at hand. In Afghanistan, she oversaw teams who engineered grain silos to reduce the substantial losses to insects and rot. In Nigeria, the focus was on warehouses and transportation. Others worked on simple fixes like getting Kenyan farmers to use crates instead of burlap bags to transport tomatoes to prevent them from bruising.

Meanwhile, Nevaeh volunteered to head up the group of the Ejected tackling the "ugly produce" problem, or food deemed too imperfect or misshapen to be consumed. She felt connected to things and people that were mislabeled, as she felt she was her entire life. Nevaeh was born with a birth defect, a disfigurement she felt people often couldn't see past. In the same way people couldn't see past the blemishes on the discarded produce. The ugly food group's efforts boosted the already existing "eat imperfect foods" movement so that it soon became mainstream. At first, retailers offered the food at deeply discounted prices. But, as people became accustomed to eating ugly food, incentives diminished.

***

Yet another Ejected group was led by Rachel, who spent her life in marketing and was previously a big proponent of bigger, flashier packaging that resulted in increased sales and a bigger end-of-year bonus. That was what got her ejected from the planet. The packaging problem perplexed Rachel's team. Implementing a garbage tax was suggested, with the reasoning that if it was so expensive to throw things away, people would demand less garbage from companies. The idea was shot down because people agreed it would take too long. They all ached to get back to their lives, and they wanted immediate results.

After several other ideas weren't well received, someone pitched a more immediate and radical approach that piqued the group's interest. The plan was to have the Ejected in invisible mode perched in front of stores across the U.S. Once the purchased packaged foods exited to the parking lot, the Ejected would grab the packaged items, rip off the packaging, and leave it in front of the entrance doors. These piles of packaging would hopefully become such a nuisance that stores would only carry products without wasteful packaging.

The plan went perfectly. Soon there were mountains of wrappers and containers in front of stores that blocked other customers from entering. The cart return workers were on the front lines. They witnessed the packaging shedding from the products and piling up in front of the entrances. They did their best to clear it away, but as soon as they got back from the dumpster, there was another pile twice the size. It didn't take long for the cart return employees all over the land to climb over mountains of trash and inform the store managers what was going on.

The store managers tended to be skeptical until they witnessed the bizarre self-forming trash mountains for themselves. They soon realized that this was probably related to the Ejected and reported the problem to the corporate headquarters. The buyers realized that this problem needed to be eliminated at its source by not allowing their vendors to sell their products in any unnecessary packaging.

Within six months, the entire supply chain changed, and packaging waste was virtually eliminated. Shampoo, conditioner, detergents, and soaps were no longer sold in plastic bottles, but rather in bars, pellets, or powders packaged in paper. Food also didn't come in packaged in plastic anymore. Instead, it was generally sold in bulk where people used their own containers or in containers that had a deposit on them. People brought the containers back to the store to be washed up and reused. If plastic was unavoidable, bioplastics were used instead.

There were unforeseen positive results from reducing the packaging. The first happy surprise was that people's health improved, since people were cooking for themselves and eating less processed food. Also, for the first time in decades, the microplastic concentrations in the oceans decreased.

Pooja was a successful food critic who loved the flavor of food cooked in wood-fired ovens or over charcoal grills. Restaurants she reviewed well thrived and the eateries that didn't please her palette usually ended up going out of business. She had a history of writing scathing reviews of establishments that opted for any cooking method that didn't deliver the smoky flavor she loved. In her long career as a critic, she never once considered the environmental impact of her preferences. She certainly wasn't trying to warm the planet, she was simply carving out a niche for herself. As a result of her unintentional damaging actions of promoting a generally more polluting way of cooking, she was now in charge of changing that.

Her team of Ejecteds worked to replace wood-fired cookstoves in villages all around the world with various types of less-polluting ones. Electric stoves powered by solar panels or wind turbines were the most common. But in some areas, the most efficient solution was to convert compostable products from farms and backyards into energy using anaerobic digestion techniques. The resulting biogas could either be converted into electricity through a generator or be used to power boilers as an alternative to natural gas. This biogas could also be upgraded to biomethane for use in heating, tractors and other road vehicles.[48]

Her team's actions helped reduced asthma and emphysema and they were on track to replace 87 million inefficient cookstoves in Asia and Africa, resulting in a reduction of 9.7 gigatons of carbon dioxide emissions.[49]

CHAPTER 17

Equitable Transportation

Bob's habit of driving everywhere had earned him the nickname "Bob the Blob." He would drive to his neighbor's house next door instead of walking across the yard or down the driveway, over a few feet, and up his neighbor's driveway. He wasn't incapable of walking; he just preferred driving. Everywhere. All the time. He also liked to do everything in person. Use Zoom for a meeting? Not a chance. He would drive two hours each way to have a twenty-minute meeting.

Aside from being *ejected* from the planet, Bob couldn't say he was surprised that there were consequences for his laziness. His wife and kids had chided him about being a ridiculous gas waster for years, until they just gave up on saying anything. They realized he wouldn't change his behaviors. Bob simply didn't think the actions of one person were a big deal.

On Bob's tour, he learned that his Land Rover that got 18 miles to the gallon emitted 4.94 pounds of CO_2e per mile.[50] Since he drove about 20,000 miles a year, his driving contributed about 98,767 pounds, or 49.4 U.S. tons, of CO_2e per year. *That is pretty heinous*, he acknowledged.

Another reason Bob ended up with the Ejected was because he was responsible for spreading false information about electric cars.

His favorite topics of conversation before his ejection revolved around denigrating electric vehicles (EVs), claiming that their manufacturing emissions were higher than normal cars and it takes electricity to run them, so those two factors negated any potential climate benefit, and they might actually be worse for the environment.

What Bob learned on his tour was that if electric cars were manufactured and powered with green electricity, they crushed combustion engines as far as carbon dioxide emissions went. Especially when their entire lifetime is considered since EVs had no tailpipe emissions. He also learned all about lithium-ion battery recycling that destroyed the lies he used to spread. Bottom line, EVs aren't perfect, but they are extremely beneficial in curbing the climate crisis.

***

Continuing from COVID, people were still encouraged to work from home whenever possible. But on top of minimizing the spread of the virus that still lingered in society, working from home was part of the climate crisis national emergency plan to reduce commuting emissions. Workplaces were required to comply with requests to work from home if the worker could produce the agreed-upon deliverables. Employers were delighted to find out that their employees were generally more productive and that morale was at an all-time high.

In case people couldn't work from home, sustainable transportation options were important. Bob knew the next step in reducing transportation miles was to strengthen pedestrian zones and bike paths—especially in low-income areas. In the United States, pedestrian and cycle-friendly areas had been concentrated in wealthy communities, leaving out low-income families and many people of color.[51]

Bob put in bike lanes and delivered bikes with small batteries to people with short commutes, especially if the recipients were sorely out of shape. Notes on the bikes read, "Use this bike instead of driving. You could use the exercise. Don't worry, there is a battery you can use for the hills. Plug it in at work so you can ride home." With Bob's leadership and help from countless other Ejected, the mass transit system became faster and more convenient than driving.

If biking, walking or mass transit weren't options, ride-share apps and car sharing programs filled in transportation gaps and became very popular. Electric vehicles could be rented by the hour, day, or week. People in urban and suburban areas found that using rentable electric cars was much more cost effective than owning their own cars and car ownership became rare. People still had car access whenever they needed it, but they didn't have to buy the car, pay to park it, insure it, fill it up with gas, pay for garage space, or repair it. Communities recognized that cars were expensive, both for people and the planet. Plus, it was awesome to be able to rent the perfect sized vehicle for the occasion. Going camping? How about an SUV? Just a doing a quick trip across town for an appointment? A compact car would do the trick. Driving the neighborhood kids to a party? Well, then a minivan was a great option.

Since the American spirit is closely associated with the concepts of innovation, independence, and convenience, electric vehicle charging stations powered by renewables quickly became super accessible and even a destination location. It didn't take long before the charging station culture blossomed—literally. The nearby solar gardens and windmill farms that ran the car chargers had beautiful trails that were planted with native flowers, shrubs, and trees.

Bob found that urban planners were eager to implement the walkable towns that they had dreamed of creating in grad-school instead of the soulless sprawling strip mall-y growth they had grown accustomed to. These town centers were also charging stations, so they brought in tourism dollars, too. Charging stations were fun places to be and had something for everyone. Not only were charging station town centers local economy hubs, but they also were cultural hubs, with restaurants, bars, coffee shops, and even spiritual centers. They encouraged a relaxed, fun, accepting, community-centered, compassionate culture where people naturally tended to consider the common good before thinking of themselves. If a person was kind and left the place in as good of shape or better than they found it, they were welcome in the community.

Road trips looked different within this way of life; a stop to refuel was no longer a five-minute affair just to stop to use the bathroom and buy gas, but rather a part of the journey. People became accustomed to stopping for an hour to charge cars with high-speed chargers and check out local shops and restaurants and hang out to enjoy their favorite beverage.

As access to transportation became equal to all members of society, incomes started leveling out. *Social equality through transportation,* thought Bob. *I'm moving people to a better standard of living.* He felt good about his new role.

CHAPTER 18

Ubuntu

Ricky would describe himself as a regular guy. He grew up in Tulsa, Oklahoma, and never considered traveling or living anywhere else. He liked the outdoors, NASCAR, loud trucks, football, and guns—so did his friends. He was proud to be an American and believed he was more American than people who were not born in the United States. Even though his schooling had ended after getting his GED when he was nineteen years old, he believed he deserved a higher standard of living than immigrants, refugees, people of color, and people with disabilities, despite not having any special skills or qualifications to enable him to earn higher wages. Ricky's feelings of inferiority to people he perceived to be above him on the social ladder made him cling even tighter to the belief that he was innately superior to other social groups he categorized as being beneath him.

Although he had a lot of national pride, he was leery of government overreach that might limit his freedoms and was against any ideas that didn't mirror his own. He made statements like, "The government needs to keep their hands off my Medicare," not understanding that Medicare was a government program. In general, he saw laws as suggestions that only applied to other people, whereas he could pick and choose which rules he wanted to follow, especially regarding the environment.

If he didn't follow every environmental regulation to the letter—or at all—he didn't think it was a big deal. *It's a big world with lots of resources that don't really need protection,* he thought. *The whole environmental thing is just a bunch of unhappy liberal doomsayers who love big government and want to take away personal freedoms.* He agreed with his neighbors that environmentalism was all fake news designed to make people feel badly.

Upon arrival at the Ejected realm and after hearing Seth lecture about everyone's environmental sins, Ricky surveyed the crowd and immediately thought that there must have been some kind of mistake. *Why am I being blamed for the world's problems? I'm a common-sense appliance delivery guy who believes in upholding what's important. And even if I haven't done everything perfectly, I'm clearly not as guilty as that highfalutin oil guy in the business suit.*

After his tour, his Defender of the Future, Sabrina, made it obvious to Ricky that his years of vocal climate denial and confusing climate and weather were enough to earn him a place with the Ejected. The constant badgering and heckling of his coworkers from other countries didn't help matters. But what sealed the deal was something Ricky thought was only between him and his maker. He had occasionally dumped truckloads of old fridges and air conditioners illegally instead of delivering them to the recycling facility. *The recycling facility was so far away,* he'd reason, *I'd waste more gas driving there.* He couldn't see any pollution coming from refrigerators and air conditioners, so he chocked it up to liberal hysteria imposing senseless and harmful rules on industry. On his tour, he was surprised to find out that most of the U.S. abided by the refrigerant recycling laws. He just assumed that everyone was like him and was trying to skirt the laws at every opportunity.

Sabrina showed him that the most pressing problems were in developing countries where they had stockpiles of old refrigerators that had been banned decades ago with the Montreal Protocol because of the harmful effects on the ozone layer. As it turned out, he learned that chlorofluorocarbons, or CFCs, don't only harm the ozone, but they also are incredibly destructive greenhouse gases. In fact, a single molecule of CFC-12 can hold nearly 11,000 times the heat of CO_2,[52] making CFC-12 an extraordinarily potent greenhouse gas.

Ricky's reaction to that was, "Well, God daaa... Bless America and all her ships at sea!" He then realized that he had, indeed, done great damage and reparations were in order.

What really moved Ricky was watching what the world would look like for his kids and his grandchildren if things didn't change. Even though he didn't have any kids yet, he hoped to at some point. They would be stuck in a world where people could hardly go outside because it was too hot most of the time. His favorite hunting areas and fishing holes were filled with insects spreading diseases that he had never heard of—much worse than the Zika virus. He loved his lifestyle and saw that future generations wouldn't have the chance to enjoy the best things in life if things didn't change. It just wasn't fair to the future.

As a member of the Ejected, Ricky now combed through developing countries to find old CFC cylinders that looked like they could be recycled instead of delivering refrigerators and air conditioners. The containers looked like small propane tanks, and they weren't easy to find. On his first mission, after quite a few pointers from Sabrina, he found a 30,000-pound cache in a small shed in Ghana.[53] If those CFCs would have been released into the atmosphere, it would have been equivalent to the CO_2 emissions from burning sixteen million gallons of gasoline.[54] If just left there, they would continue to slowly leak.

He peered into the shed and the importance of this delivery overwhelmed him. He paced around in small circles in front of the shed, shouting obscenities trying to get the nerve up to start the process of getting these tanks recycled. When he finally gained his composure, he carefully packaged the canisters and personally delivered them to European state-of-the-art CFC recycling facilities.

As he continued combing through African countries in the search of CFCs, he watched how people lived and interacted with one another. He was amazed by the warmth he felt as people welcomed him with open arms into their community instead of the suspicion he was used to.

He saw communities working together for the common good. When there was a crop failure, it wasn't only the farmer's problem. It was the community's collective problem, and the community worked together to solve it and feed everyone. He watched social groups celebrate everyone's uniqueness and recognize each person played an important part in the community. *I have to say, it seems like a really nice life, with a lot less anger, judgment, and fear than the town where I live.*

This new worldview piqued his curiosity and, in his free time, he studied Ubuntuism, a political philosophy that encourages community equality and a more equal distribution of wealth. The underlying philosophy could be summarized with "I am because we are" or "humanity towards others." He saw parallels between Ubuntuism and socialism and communism, but he liked Ubuntu better because he didn't see it as a system where some undeserving people got free handouts or that everyone was treated exactly the same. He saw people working together and using their talents to make the world a better place. He liked that everyone had value and no one needed to feel inferior to anyone. Most importantly, there wasn't a class of people left behind—the way he and his friends often felt.

He especially liked the redemption part of the philosophy that relates to how people deal with "errant, deviant, and dissident members of the community"—*basically, my friends,* he thought. This society does not throw out members of society, but instead seeks to redeem community members who have gone astray.

CHAPTER 19

Lifting Up Women

To improve the lives and statuses of girls and women, this group's members came from all over the world, from a wide range of backgrounds and from every social class. What all of these people had in common, though, was how they had contributed to holding women down in some way. The group was made up of mostly males, but there were some female perpetrators as well.

Their Defender, Aziza, explained, "In just 170 years, the population has grown from 1.2 billion to 7.6 billion people. Back in 1850, it took about 75 years to add a billion people. Now, we're adding a billion people every 12 years. Population and rising consumption rates are the drivers of all environmental problems. So, to get at one of the root causes, we have to stabilize population growth."

This group of Ejected just stared blankly at Aziza, completely missing the connection that limiting women's rights was directly connected to increased population. They needed it spelled out for them.

"When women have basic rights, such as the right to own, inherit, and manage property; get a divorce; obtain credit; get an education; and participate in the community and political matters, they are able to support themselves. They also tend to postpone childbearing and have fewer children, compared with women who are denied these rights.[55] When opportunities—like getting an education—are limited, how will women support themselves? And who will take care of them when they are old? Children are often seen as those women's 401(k) and retirement plan," explained Aziza.

***

Mohammed Munir discriminated against women, but he didn't think he did. He considered himself to be a defender of the faith by enforcing his strict interpretation of Islamic law. Namely, he still stood by banning girls from going to school.

***

Phil Bellman discriminated against women too. Although he didn't think he did, either—especially after he met Mohammed. After all, Phil never had anything to do with limiting women's and girls' education, or their right to own property or anything like that.

Phil's discrimination was much subtler. He just avoided hiring women in their childbearing years because he didn't want to potentially pay for maternity leave. One time, he denied one of his part-time employees her maternity leave, even though she was ordered by her physician to be on bedrest until the baby came. He just told her that she better hope to have the baby on a Friday because she'd be expected to be back at work the following Monday.

In general, he gave women a hard time for being late or needing time off, assuming it was always kid-related, even if the women didn't have children. With the men in the office, he looked the other way when it came to tardiness. If men didn't keep regular schedules, especially if it was for doing something manly, like going hunting, he'd never make it an issue.

When guys in the office had kids, they usually received a bonus or a raise soon after the big event to help them provide for their family. But Phil never thought new mothers deserved a raise. He'd embarrass women and accuse them of stealing company time when he would "catch" them "sneaking off" to pump their breast milk on their earned and required-by-law breaks. Overall, women were just "distractible" in Phil's view, and not "team players" when they didn't pick up last-minute shifts because of trouble arranging child care logistics.

***

Wei and Fang Huang were a married couple that ended up being partners in crime as well. For over a decade, they had been luring Chinese girls and young women into the sex industry. They hadn't planned on being career sex traffickers; they'd sort of gotten trapped in the business. When they first got into the business, it was going to be a one-time job to help them pay for an apartment. But, when the money came easily, they agreed to do another job. Before they knew it, they had become so intertwined with extremely well-organized and dangerous criminal gangs, there was really no way out. Even if they quit, the gangs would find them and get their revenge.

Wei and Fang typically recruited girls and women from rural areas by offering them jobs that didn't really exist in cities. Their trafficking ring worked like clockwork, with each member having different positions and earning a good wage for their specialized duties. Fang would earn the girls' and women's trust, then tell them about a promising "job opportunity." She would give the women and girls Wei's business card. Wei would conduct a "phone interview" and hire them on the spot for the fictitious job in the city. He would then offer transportation that made the victims feel very special and appreciated.

When these girls and young women arrived in the city, they would only then find out about the large travel fees they now owed and that they would have to be sex workers to pay that money back. If the girls and women they were luring into being sex workers tried to leave, they would confiscate the victims' passports, imprison them, or even physically threaten them.

***

One by one, this huge group of Ejected started lifting women up to get them on more equal footing with men. Often these actions were subtle, like just allowing a woman to speak without being interrupted.

On a grander scale, Phil, Wei and Fang, as well as innumerable other Ejected, were posted at the United Nations to implement policies that had been created decades ago but never implemented. These broad policies included educating women, giving women rights and freedom to make choices about their own bodies, and empowering women to make the choices that were best for them.

After much inner struggle, Mohammed Munir came to realize that his faith and educating woman didn't conflict as he had previously believed. He led a group of Ejected in putting in wells so that girls wouldn't have to spend their lives carrying water to their villages. Instead, these girls could now attend school and build futures for themselves by learning trades, skills, and professions. If children were something they desired to have, they had that option, but it was no longer their only option.

CHAPTER 20

Flat Stanley

Most people would describe Stanley as a nice enough guy, but not super bright and *wow*, was he ever *skinny*. He'd gotten the nickname "Flat Stanley" on the basketball court in middle school by his teammate Calvin, who remembered the classic children's book series in which the flattened Stanley character made the best of his predicament by sliding under doors, traveling via U.S. mail in an envelope, and so on. The nickname stuck with Stanley for the rest of his life.

Some unkind people called him "flat-lining Stanley" because, well, again, he wasn't too smart. One of his favorite topics of conversation was supposedly debunking climate science by "proving" that climate change was caused by natural occurrences, such as volcanic eruptions, even though, in reality, volcanoes are only responsible for less than one percent of the annual emissions.[56] His denial and ignorance of actual science was what got Stanley ejected and landed him in the other realm.

Unfortunately, even after he was shown on his tour what the reality was, he had a hard time processing the information. His Defender wanted to teach him that volcanoes were, indeed, a small contributor, but wildfires were a real and substantial contributor. Understanding wildfires was nuanced and a bit more complicated, because although it was true that wildfires are naturally occurring, the warming planet is making conditions for wildfires more favorable, with higher temperatures, stronger winds, and lower humidity in certain regions like the Arctic, the Amazon, California, and Australia.

Stanley's takeaway was that climate change was caused by wildfires, not humans. Unfortunately, the finer details were too much for Flat Stanley's intellect, and he never did grasp the situation. The Defenders eventually gave up on him. Although they didn't believe it was impossible to work with him, they felt the pressure of time and knew that it would take a lot of patience to teach Stanley what he needed to know.

The only way Stanley would ever get back to Earth would be if he was carried by the others' efforts because he wasn't assigned a mission and never realized he wasn't pulling his weight. The rest of the Ejected realized this about Stanley, but also realized that sometimes people just needed to pick up the slack for others. After all, he was a decent guy with a good heart.

CHAPTER 21

Campfire Girls

Speaking of good hearts, Eve and Esther were sisters who volunteered on a regular basis for the animal shelter on Main Street. They also enjoyed baking and handing out their goods to people on street corners.

Eve and Esther's favorite pastime was having bonfire, and they had one nearly every night. They loved how a campfire brought friends and family together like few other activities did. Staring into the fire, talking, and singing (mostly church songs) was something they never tired of and they were not looking to stop.

Little did they realize the impact of their relentless kumbaya lifestyle on their neighbors who were too polite to complain. Their campfires released a surprisingly large number of pollutants, including: nitrogen oxides, carbon monoxide, particulate matters, benzene, as well as other potentially toxic volatile organic compounds (VOCs), and, of course, carbon dioxide.

Right next door to Eve and Esther, lived a little boy named Timmy who had cystic fibrosis. He often had to come in early from playing because of the smoke. Timmy's mother wanted to embrace the live and let live mentality, but these young women had fires every single night. *Don't they have any other hobbies or obligations?* she wondered.

When Eve and Esther learned about the negative impacts of their bonfires on their tour, they felt terrible. They'd never meant to hurt anyone. They decided that fires were still a profoundly human experience that spans time and culture, so they made a solar-powered campfire that flickered realistically and gave off heat too. Its popularity spread like, well, wildfire.

CHAPTER 22

The Tally

Nearly nine months had passed and the Ejected all gathered with the Defenders in the realm to find out the impacts of their changes. Would their actions be enough to bring them back to Earth? The Ejected and the Defenders all cheered as they watched the needles steadily drop. People began dancing, high-fiving, hugging, and doing back flips. The realm's lack of gravity certainly had its upsides. They all knew that the falling needles meant they'd be able to return to their loved ones soon! As the festivities were getting revved up, an alarm sounded that ruined the celebratory mood. The needle shook for what seemed like forever before it started to rise. The Ejected looked to the Defenders for clarification. The Defenders looked at each other with wide eyes and panicked expressions, asking one another, "What's happening?"

The Defender in charge of GPS, Mikael, reacted by checking the dashboard and pinpointing the problems' origins. The Ejected instinctively held their breath and waited for an explanation as Mikael and Aziza took charge.

"There's a war breaking out over oil supplies in the Middle East," announced Mikael. "With increased pressure on their already under-supported medical system, they will lose access to health care and family planning measures, like birth control. The population will rise steeply. And we know population growth is a major issue at the crux of our warming Earth."

"We need to stop this war from breaking out," declared Keith. Then he asked, "What is the cause of the war?"

"The desire to control valuable oil and gas assets to increase national power," answered Aziza.

"But the world is decarbonizing," Keith replied. "Why are those oil reserves still valuable?"

Mikael explained, "Because about twenty percent of the world's population isn't going along with the majority and decarbonizing their economies. This minority population is led by the fossil fuel industries that want to keep fossil fuels the status quo so they can keep making a ton of money. They don't want to have to spend even a nickel on investing in green energy. They'd rather just make more money despite the consequences. These fossil fuel barons are skilled at tapping into people's greed and self-interest, and they have constructed a narrative that appeals to these folks' deepest fears. The fossil fuel tycoons sow seeds of anger, judgment, discontent, and misinformation among these people who already feel their concerns are being ignored."

"Who are these people? And what are they afraid of?" asked Rachel.

"They are mostly right-wing populists," answered Aziza.

"What's a populist?" asked Ricky.

"The general term describes a political approach that appeals to ordinary people who feel that their concerns are ignored by the established power," explained Aziza. "Populists see themselves as the good people who believe in personal freedom above all else. They oppose the corrupt and self-serving elite, whom they see as always trying to limit their freedoms. The populists generally don't have any education past high school and are fiercely nationalistic. As a whole, they usually don't like change or traveling and they are content to stay where they are. Another characteristic of populists is that they don't seek to understand other people's points of view. They tend to think their way of thinking about things is the only valid way to consider the world."

Ricky said, "Hey! You just described my friends. They ain't as bad as they sound!"

With that statement, Ricky nominated himself to change his friends' minds.

CHAPTER 23

The Protesters

When Ricky arrived at the carbon tax protest in front of the capitol building, he saw his friends scattered throughout the crowd. They wanted their inexpensive oil back, and to them, the matter wasn't any more complicated than that. It was a common-sense, black-and-white issue for them—cheaper was better. They didn't want the price of gas and other petroleum-based products to potentially go up. Besides, they liked their powerful, loud, and smelly trucks, and it just didn't seem masculine to have quiet electric trucks.

The protest vibe was fearful and angry. The societal changes that the crowd had already witnessed rattled them. *Oil=Freedom*, read a protester's sign.

Ricky was puzzled by the sign. *Why do they think oil paves the way for freedom? That's actually backwards,* he thought. *Governments with economies based on oil do not need to tax their people in order to survive. They can simply drill an oil well and ignore their citizens' wishes.*[57]

And here's a classic sign, thought Ricky. It read, *Go big or go home!* and had a picture of a monster truck on it.

There were also signs telling various groups of people to go back to where they came from and that real Americans needed the help first. Ricky didn't know what exactly was meant by helping real Americans first, but he figured that it was a nod to the fact that the poorest communities' houses had been made energy efficient first—and that probably included immigrant families. Ricky assumed correctly that those signs represented a feeling that this group of protesters resented that people they considered beneath them received assistance and fancy new houses that they didn't deserve. Ricky knew that facts didn't matter to most of the people attending this protest. What mattered to them was that, if something felt true, it was true.

As Ricky walked through the crowd, gathering up his friends, Jesse greeted him enthusiastically. "Ricky! Where in Sam Hill have you been?"

This was followed by a beaming, "Well, I'll be," from Billy Ray and a quiet, "Good to see ya," from Earl, who gave him a manly one-second, one-armed hug that felt more like a slap.

Otis heard about Ricky's arrival and came looking for him. He approached the group exclaiming, "Well, butter my butt and call me a biscuit! Ricky's back! Where ya been? We thought you were dead!" Otis loved throwing in his colorful southern statements, and his friends came to rely on his sayings for entertainment.

Ricky grinned at his buddies. It was so good to see their familiar faces. He had known most of these guys since elementary school. The jokes and ribbing carried over from those formative years, but the level of humor never changed. He assured everyone that it was really him and that he was the same ol' Ricky. Ricky began explaining to his friends that he was one of the Ejected, when Roscoe interrupted him.

"Why, no ya ain't," interrupted Roscoe, "There ain't no Ejected, Ricky. That's just the liberal media making it all up."

"Yeah, it's all a hoax," agreed Tiny, who clearly was given the nickname to express irony.

Ricky answered, "I'm telling y'all. It's *not* a hoax. I got ejected from the planet and have been in another realm. Climate science is real. Climate change is happening, and burning fossil fuels is the root cause."

His friends reacted with utter silence until Bo declared, "Look who's gotten too big for his britches!"

"Dern tootin'," agreed Earl.

Tiny joined his friends, explaining in a little louder voice as if Ricky just wasn't hearing him, "No, Ricky. It ain't like that. It's just that those liberals are making a whole lot of nothing out some science mumbo jumbo that the planet's warming. It ain't true, Ricky. Just like dinosaurs ain't true."

"Yeah, Ricky," interjected Harlan, "We don't want a carbon tax that makes everything more expensive. Why would we be for something that'll cost us more money?"

"Harlan," Ricky explained, "it might cost y'all a little more for the next few years, but think about how much it'll cost the next generation if we don't change. If you stick with oil, you're taking away the next generation's future."

His friends were silent, so Ricky felt he needed to explain himself better. He detailed what he saw on his tour and how kids, not too far into the future, couldn't go hunting and fishing because of the warming planet that allowed so many new viruses to thrive. He ended the story by explaining how he couldn't return to the planet unless this carbon tax stayed in place.

Ricky waited for the others to instantly, enthusiastically, and unanimously agree to uphold the carbon tax. But they didn't. Instead, they all looked around in silence, avoiding eye contact with each other, and especially with Ricky. Their indifference to Ricky's return filled him with sadness and anger. He'd thought these people were his friends! Wasn't the choice obvious? Ricky shook his head and walked away so others wouldn't see the tears filling his eyes.

It occurred to Ricky that he was a different person now, and maybe he didn't even want to return to Oklahoma. These people weren't really his friends, not if they were choosing their trucks over him. Then he thought, *And they aren't even good people if they are choosing their trucks over the future.* He wondered, *How can they be so selfish, and why don't they believe in science?*

But as soon as that thought entered his mind, he had to chuckle. *Have I forgotten where I came from? Of course, my friends don't believe in science. Science was for uppity people who were, in their minds, automatically rivals to them because of their higher social statuses. It didn't matter what those scientists had to say—these rednecks resented them and believed the people spewing scientific facts had an ulterior motive to hold them down somehow and for some inexplicable reason.* He remembered his own upbringing and how he had been exactly like his friends before he entered the realm. His grandma always told him that the only science he needed to know was right in the Bible—and he never actually read that.

His anger softened, and he realized that what his friends all shared was a life story of real or imagined unfairness and anxiety, stagnation, falling social status, shame, and need. It didn't actually matter to them if their claims were real or made up on the spot. Ricky concluded again that what mattered to them was that if something felt true, it was true.

Ricky turned back around and said, "I guess I'm not the same person I was before I disappeared, after all. I've evolved."

"Like a Pokémon?" asked Mack.

"Um, well, yeah. Sort of. I mean, no. What are you talking about? I'm not a fictional character," replied Ricky, "I just mean, I'm still Ricky, but I feel like I'm a better version of myself now, and I don't want to go back to my old ways. I wasn't happy. I drank too much. If there was a problem in my life, I looked for someone to blame it on. Looking back, I guess I was depressed. But now I'm helping the world truly be a better place, and I feel good about it. I figured out that if I can't find the sunshine, I hafta *be* the sunshine. Sometimes I need to be the sunshine for others. Just because. Without expecting anything in return. I don't worry about if things are 'fair' or not like I used to. And then, eventually, sunshine is all around me because others are sharing theirs."

"Solar panels? Are we talkin' solar panels now?" asked Mack, struggling to understand Ricky's metaphor.

"Seriously, Mack," said Ricky, "I'm a little worried about you."

"Y'all are after the American Dream—you know the idea that, if you work hard and play by the rules, you can have a better life. But what happens when that dream doesn't come true? Huh, Travis? You've had lots of hard knocks…and they ain't your fault. It's OK to receive those government programs for a while until you get back up on your feet. We don't fault ya for it. But other folks, ya know, they've been hit hard, too. They ain't any less of people for needing help, too," explained Ricky.

Now Ricky was on a roll and couldn't stop himself, "And, Buzz, you always seem to think some people are cutting in line and getting ahead while you ain't going nowhere. I hate to be so blunt, but maybe you should consider quitting the habitual day drinking. You might get yerself ahead."

His friends stared at Ricky, so he took the opportunity to continued, "And remember when we used to make fun of the Mexicans and then Juan showed up and became one of us?" reminisced Ricky.

"But he's been here for twenty years. Juan's different," said Jesse.

"Yeah," cracked Otis, "and his English is better 'n yours, Jesse!" Everyone laughed. Jesse would never live down the sign he'd made in fourth grade that read "moth wadring peetsa" for the school carnival pizza booth.

"But, Jesse, how do we know the other Mexican workers, not to mention the Somali and Hmong workers, aren't cool too?" asked Ricky.

"Y'all don't seem to realize that big oil only cares about big oil. They ain't actually interested in keeping your life affordable. The only thing they care about is selling more fossil fuels and making more money for themselves," said Ricky, "They also don't care that they're polluting the air that's giving the kids asthma and other medical problems. How many of you have kids with asthma?" Several of them nodded, indicating they did.

Ricky knew he was on a soap box and that he was teetering on pushing his friends away with his preachiness, but he felt he had to continue. "Y'all are so afraid that someone's gonna take something away from you that you rarely ever give anything first. That's actually what I like about living in that carbon-conscious society. People just… help each other. There's no need for people to steal meat from people's freezers, Buck."

"Wait," said Buck, "you knew that was me?"

"Hell, yeah," Ricky responded, "We all did, right?" Everyone nodded in agreement.

Embarrassed, Buck said, "I'm sorry, I just saw your freezer so full, I thought you wouldn't mind if I grabbed a couple…"

Ricky interrupted, "We didn't mind, Buck. That's why we never said nothing. We knew your family needed food. But I just wished I would've acknowledged the situation and had given you some meat instead of ignoring it and making you feel ashamed for having to do it."

"Like do what Jesus would do?" offered Mack.

"Yeah, a lot of those crunchy granola-loving liberals got beards just like Jesus too," joked Roscoe.

"Hey," hollered Tiny, who had a ZZ Top-style beard, "you ain't knockin' beards, are ya?"

"No, of course not, Tiny," said Roscoe with a laugh.

"Lots of ponytails, too, then?" asked Mack.

"And man buns, I bet," said Travis thoughtfully.

"I draw the line at man buns," Roscoe announced, with his arms up like he was surrendering.

Ricky saw the conversation getting off track and steered the conversation back. "The carbon-conscious people don't judge ya for what kind of job you have. They embrace diversity and expect that everyone is doing the best they can. They realize that sometimes people might look like a big environmental sinner in some ways but make up for it in other ways. They celebrate differences in people instead of fearing them. They care for each other. You'd like it. There's a place for all of your goofy selves there."

"Hell, I met lots of 'green' rednecks, too. You'd fit right in with some of them who like tanning deer hides. But the big difference is that those carbon-conscious rednecks are peaceful, not always angry about everything and afraid something'll cramp their style or someone will take something away from them. People just sort of share stuff and show up at your door with stuff. Kind of the way we used to do around here when we were growing up. Y'all gotta stop hating outsiders. Your life moves in the direction of your strongest thoughts, and if all you're doing is hatin' everyone for everything, your life is gonna be filled with hate and anger. It's not serving you…or the world," asserted Ricky.

"In order to win the climate crisis," Ricky continued without taking a breath, "every single person on the planet needs to work together. We can't keep dividing people up into arbitrary groups—liberals, conservatives, immigrants, fat people, old people, dark people, light people, smart people, ugly people, beautiful people, or whatever—and finding faults in everyone. We've all got faults. But it's time to stop looking for our differences and start looking for our commonalities. We all want a bright future. And you guys are the enemy to the rest of the world right now because you're against the future because all you're interested in is yourselves and the little bit of sacrifice this might potentially cost you. Why do you even think this is all about you? Besides, do y'all even realize that no one is even talking about raising taxes for you guys? The increase will be paid for by the extremely wealthy and it won't cramp their fancy lifestyles even one little bit."

Ricky had the floor and everyone was listening, so he wasn't about to stop now. "If y'all hate people controlling you, then stop being so dependent on oil. That's like nestling up with a snake in the grass. I know y'all are worried these changes are gonna leave you behind, but I tell ya. Don't let yourselves be left behind. They have free training for those solar installer jobs and also for electric vehicle mechanics. And it's better pay than you're making now. I tell ya, there's a place for you in the new world order."

"I guess you *have* evolved, Ricky," reflected Harlan, "And maybe we should, too." Ricky surveyed his friends, who looked at each other with sideways glances. Ricky thought, *OK. They're coming around.*

Then Roscoe hollered, "Who'd rather go fishing than be here?" and he started heading for his truck. The rest of the gang followed. That action told Ricky that they agreed with him, but they'd probably never talk about it.

CHAPTER 24

The Betrayal

Keith thought he could help stop the carbon tax from being repealed by visiting his longtime friend Brian, a fellow oil guy, who was intricately connected in Washington, D.C. He wanted to explain to Brian why the carbon tax was needed and why it was truly the best way to slow the world's carbon output. However, the discussion didn't go as planned.

It didn't help that Keith showed up unannounced because when Brian is startled, his go-to "fight or flight" response was fight. Brian started off angry and couldn't shake it. As soon as Keith told Brian that he was behind the carbon tax, Brian became enraged.

"You betrayed me, Keith! How could you think a carbon tax could be a good idea? I'll lose money!" shouted Brian.

Keith answered emphatically, "But it's not just about you, Brian. It's about the future. I've seen the future, and it looks grim if fossil fuels continue to be used at the rate they are being used now."

"Oh, you've *seen* the future, huh?" chided Brian. "Yeah, because that's possible."

"Brian, I'm a giant, glowing Tinkerbell," said Keith as he realized he *still* hadn't mastered the visibility settings, "and you're having a conversation with me. I'm telling you, I have access to insights you don't, and I'm telling you as a colleague, a friend, and a fellow dad, do this for Lisa and Benjamin. Ben has diabetes. Diabetes increases sensitivity to heat stress. You need to invest in renewables now for the health of the future. You'll still be rich as hell, and you won't hate yourself."

 Brian just stared at Keith without saying a word, did an about-face, and walked away without looking back.

Crushed, Keith had to think of a new plan. He couldn't believe he'd been unable to change Brian's mind. *Is money really more powerful than the love a parent feels for their children?*

He hoped that Ricky was having more luck with his mission. He was disappointed with how things went with Brian, but it gave him hope knowing Ivy and Jayla connected with other social media cultural influencers, and *#livingsimply* was becoming mainstream quickly. The lifestyle sold itself; no need to present facts to show how working less and enjoying life more was appealing. Who wouldn't want a more enjoyable life, with meaningful work that gave people a sense of purpose? Maybe that would be enough. He prayed it would be.

CHAPTER 25

Last-Ditch Efforts

Ricky was suddenly sucked back into the realm. *Well, I guess my job there is done, then,* he thought. *It sure would be nice if I'd get a little warning, though.* The other Ejected greeted him with cheers, whistles, and applause. It was an entrance he could get used to. All of the Ejected gathered around the needles and gauges to see where the CO_2e levels were and if the drop in CO_2e would be enough for them to go back to Earth. Each of them missed their loved ones so much it hurt to breathe. They had to get back. They watched nervously and celebrated as Ricky's needle kept moving down. The joyous mood came to an abrupt halt as people realized that even though all these pieces were in place, it was still going to take some more time. The Ejected weren't going back to Earth anytime soon.

A wave of disappointment swept across the realm and the heart-broken Ejected didn't try to mask their sadness. Keith stepped up and announced, "OK, I know this is disappointing, but instead of stopping and waiting, now is the time to put our heads together and think of some low-hanging fruit that will quickly move the needles. Ideas?"

Without missing a beat, as if she'd been waiting for the question her whole life, a tiny, old woman named Kyung-ja said, "We could save a hundred million trees that serve as nice carbon sinks by stopping the production of junk mail. Stopping junk mail would be like taking nine million cars off the road, or heating thirteen million homes in the winter.[58] How about we make ninja stars out of the junk mail and throw it all back at the mail carriers?"

No one could believe what they were hearing. Other Ejected asked themselves, *Does Kyung-ja always walk around with facts like this ready to go? Even though it was a crazy idea, it wasn't dull.*

When this sweet old grandma-like lady realized she still had the floor, she continued talking as she began folding paper. "Throwing paper ninja stars at mail carriers wouldn't hurt them, but it would scare them. Since we'd be in invisible mode, all they would see would be paper that was apparently folding itself up and then hurling itself back at them." Then she made burly Seth flinch as she hurled her newly formed ninja star at him. Everyone laughed.

Seth ran the junk mail reduction efforts through the simulator model and found that it still wasn't quite enough, but it would help. A large group of the eagerly Ejected volunteered to go down to Earth to carry out this fun mission. The Ejected who had experience with the invisibility mode that shed packaging and left it in front of stores were chosen first.

Upon arrival, they waited in invisible mode by mailboxes to ambush unsuspecting mail carriers. The mail carriers were, indeed, freaked out by the self-making ninja stars that followed them through neighborhoods. Mail carriers drove recklessly, looking more in their rearview mirrors than through their windshields, in an effort to escape the junk mail ninja stars. As for those that delivered mail on foot, they trampled gardens as they ran, looking over their shoulders, desperately trying to escape the inexplicable origami mobs. One embarrassed mail carrier was discovered tangled up in a clothesline with underwear on her head.

Irate neighbors complained loudly to the postal service that their mail carriers were a menace. Mail carriers denied the allegations and blamed the problem on junk mail, which they then refused to deliver.

Within a few weeks, junk mail was banned from being delivered by the U.S. Postal Service, and organizations and businesses adjusted their outreach methods appropriately. Junk mail soon became a thing of the past and kind of a dirty word.

***

"What else can we do?" asked Nevaeh.

"Although doing things online rather than in person radically reduces the transportation footprint, it isn't footprint free," chimed in Mike, an IT guy from Texas. "Every time we use a search engine, there's an output of greenhouse gases because every unique search requires multiple servers.[59] One Google search creates between 0.2-7 grams of CO_2 emissions, which is the equivalent of driving a car 52 feet.[60]

And a single email has a footprint of four grams of CO_2. Just think about all of those unnecessary reply-all emails that are sent every day. They not only annoy the people who don't need to be on that email chain, but they are also actually causing pollution by wasting energy." With that information, the Ejected started stealing sideways glances at each other to see if others felt a little guilt about this, too.

Mike explained, "The information communications and technology industry, including internet, social media, streaming, and cloud services, currently produces about two percent of global CO_2 emissions, which is more than air travel."[61] We could reduce this impact by approaching the issue from two different sides. First, we should delete the nonessential information that is being stored. We should start with big files—like obsolete videos—and then tackle things like people's inboxes. No one needs their emails from five years ago, despite what they might think. Second, we should switch cloud servers and data center servers to exclusively using green energy."

A large group of the Ejected started looking through files to purge, and the next day, millions of people felt physically lighter when their digital footprint didn't weigh as much. Somehow the digital baggage was felt by their souls. People just seemed happier and they didn't miss the files.

∗∗∗

The remaining group felt a little useless until Doris offered, "We could unplug everything that is plugged in or in standby mode."

The group collectively responded, "Why?"

Doris explained that appliances and gadgets were "phantom energy users" because they still use small bits of energy. "Unplugging everything when not in use will reduce one percent of the global carbon dioxide," she explained.[62]

The immediate consensus was that doing this was a no-brainer. In a moment, the Ejected covered the Earth, unplugging practically every electronic device that was still plugged into a wall socket, but not in use since it was still continuing to consume electricity even after it was switched off. Phone chargers, laptop power adaptors, microwave ovens, game consoles, and CD and DVD players were all being unplugged if they weren't being used.

The needle started to vibrate, then started to drop. Little by little, it went down.

That was enough! Cheers erupted and, as people turned to congratulate each other, they disappeared from the realm.

CHAPTER 26

A Taste of Solidarity

Keith surprised Ivy and Viola by appearing in their living room. This time he was visible, but not glowing. He was back to normal.

"DAD!" shrieked Ivy as she jumped up from the couch and over the coffee table to reach him. She hugged him tighter than she'd ever hugged anyone before. Tears streamed down both of their faces.

Keith's body shook as he cried and felt the extraordinary love and calm that seemed to penetrate right down to his DNA. Viola glided across the room with outstretched arms and sank into Keith and Ivy as she wrapped her arms around both of them.

"You're back," whispered Viola, "I finally feel like I can breathe again."

Keith answered, "I am back. Not just physically, but mentally and spiritually, too."

Ivy knew her mom and dad were meant to be together. She always knew she wasn't in denial.

★★★

Heather sobbed as she scooped up her boys and squeezed them tight. Her boys squealed, "Mama! Mama!" over and over and she couldn't stop kissing their soft, squishy cheeks.

She was so happy to finally let go of her anger and feeling like she needed to keep score of rights and wrongs. She knew she would forever miss Jason, but she also knew she needed to focus on appreciating what she had. She had so many blessings. She resolved to share her gifts, talents, love, and abundance with others.

***

Doris was welcomed home with a parade on First Avenue put together only hours after the town heard of her arrival. She was humbled when the town elected her honorary mayor because she knew it was the entire Midwest that deserved the credit of changing their practices, not just her. She was proud to be a farmer. The act of planting a crop upheld the virtues of faith and hope. And mother nature was sure to keep other potential deadly sins like pride and idleness in check.

***

Bob had lost so much weight he was barely recognizable and his family mistook him for an intruder at first. He became a sought-after spokesperson for several weight loss programs.

***

Ricky predicted his friends would be trying to hook a bass and found them at the reservoir. After a few months of hanging out with friends and family, he decided to move back to Africa. Somehow he felt more at home there than in Oklahoma, something he would have never predicted. He eventually married, had a baby girl and taught her how to fish in Lake Nasser.

***

Wei and Fang continued their international movement to stop sex trafficking and were able to reform the criminal system they were working in.

***

Phil lost his job as the boss since he was gone for so long and his absence wasn't covered under the Family Medical Leave Act. His new boss was a female employee whom he'd wronged. He gave her a heart-felt apology that she accepted. She graciously offered him a position at the company doing the job she used to do.

***

Mohammed was known for his kindness and charity to the poor through all of his actions, but especially by creating all of those wells to help women and girls have the opportunity to attend schools. He was instrumental in bringing fundamentalist and mainstream society together to find common ground. He embodied love for God and love for God's creatures, and it was almost impossible to dislike this man with twinkling brown eyes.

***

It took nearly ten months for the Ejected to return home. The date was March third, and it was unlike any other day in history. All around the world, people rejoiced and celebrated the return of the Ejected. Humanity had united around doing what was right for the world, rather than what was self-serving. It was a turning point in human history to have people acting together with a common vision of peace, equity, and long-term thinking to preserve the Earth for future generations.

Wars were halted, nitpicking diminished, and there was a concerted effort to replace passing judgment with seeking understanding, expressing compassion, and exercising tolerance. People were at peace with themselves and in harmony with those around them. It was truly an awesome and spiritual experience that was made possible by the fundamental shifts that had taken place in society, transcending religious, political, and cultural affiliations.

But after six weeks, the harmony started unravelling. After all, people have short attention spans and grew weary of the concerted effort it takes to practice self-discipline. People started slipping into old habits. They were hungry to believe the tempting disinformation that circulated in society and seemed to offer an easier path.

Democracy, civility, and truth were under siege as disinformation campaigns coupled with the complexity of carbon footprints took advantage of people's climate justice fatigue.

CHAPTER 27

Disinformation Playbook

It was a dark time as a segment of society hung on to the carbon past while others worked toward a carbon-neutral future. The division in society was corrosive. Pundits compared the times to the fall of the Berlin wall. At first there was widespread jubilation, but soon after, there was hard work to be done.

Although most companies didn't engage in disinformation campaigns, there were plenty that did. These companies sowed seeds of doubt that fueled disputes, name calling, and eventual violence. It didn't look promising for the survival of humankind as anger, blame, and self-righteousness reached new heights and democracies turned into police states arresting people without cause or warrants.

There was a segment of society that denied that people were ever ejected from the planet and were obsessed with consuming more energy than they needed. They also pushed for bigger cars and weaker mileage standards. Others factions were trying to rid of the planet of people because they wanted more resources for themselves.

Five disinformation "plays" were commonly used to deceive the public. And although companies across all business sectors engaged in strategic ploys to muddy the waters, the oil industry systematically employed all five disinformation plays to hold on to its power.

Play #1. The Diversion: Create Doubt

People started actively seeking brain-candy-type distractions as they longed for something new and easy to think about. They were mentally exhausted from sifting through so much content to figure out how to do the carbon-conscious thing. As a result, new diversion topics trended daily across social media and news platforms: a rumor of a sex scandal, a drastic change in a celebrity's weight, exposing a politician's obvious lie, streaming a binge-worthy series, discussing bizarre conspiracy theories, and so on. People were hungry for escaping the reality of the world situation and their responsibility to help. It was easier to pretend it wasn't happening.

Preying on the general distractibility and growing restlessness of society, the fossil fuels industry stepped up their already well-developed practices of manufacturing doubt and creating the appearance of uncertainty. They formed seemingly independent front groups to undermine science, influence policy, and divert the conversation from the real issues at hand.

Play #2. The Fake: Counterfeit Science

A general lack of critical thinking and weak scientific skills made it sinfully easy to confuse the American public with false or conflicting information. Articles were planted in legitimate scientific journals with skewed study results that selectively published results that supported their industry while under-reporting results that would weaken their company. Industries also commissioned scientific studies with flawed methodologies biased toward predetermined results to cloud straightforward facts. Even conscientious people, who were desperately trying to do the right thing, were duped by this fake science and people started making terrible choices. People clung to "common sense" answers that the manufactured studies "revealed." These studies appealed to people who were looking for an easy path forward and fueled new outrageous conspiracy theories that were fraught with ridiculous untruths.

Since lifestyle choices to curb climate change are very nuanced, there is no black and white, one-size fits all answer for every individual. People got caught in the trap of comparing themselves to others and pointing fingers instead of worrying about their own actions. Self-righteous people attacked others which activated peoples' powerful defensive biases—when brains protect themselves from hurtful information by rejecting it. Defensive biases made it easy for people to dismiss, deny, and distort anything that they didn't want to believe. The world started slipping back to where they were before people were ejected from the planet. And it became clear, once again, that facts don't change minds, especially when it was tricky to tell fact from fiction.

Play #3. The Blitz: Harass Scientists and Advocates

Scientists and advocates who spoke out with results or views that undermined particular industries were intimidated in many different ways: demotions, slanderous statements that tarnished reputations, defunded research, even abductions, and murder. Sneaky corporations silenced scientists through unreasonable lawsuits or requested records requests just to bury them in paperwork and waste their labor resources.

Solidarity turned to discord and ugliness. Even children like Ivy and Jayla didn't escape harassment. American politicians with cozy relationships with oil companies felt threatened by these children's influence, and attacked their character on Twitter.

Play #4. The Screen: Greenwash and Buy Credibility through Alliances

Some crafty companies also used "greenwashing" to market themselves as being part of the climate solution. In truth, they were actively working behind the scenes to undermine policies and regulations. Other companies boosted their credibility through alliances with universities or professional societies using under-handed academic alliances to influence self-serving research and spread misinformation that undermined science.

Play #5. The Fix: Manipulate Government Officials

Bribes to manipulate government officials became commonplace. These payoffs were routinely denied, despite obvious paper trails. Industry trade associations intensified their lobbying for legislation to repeal the carbon tax. It was easy for people to lose faith in their government.

CHAPTER 28

The Sweater

Ivy showed up in tears at Jayla's front door. She was attacked on Twitter again. Even though she knew she shouldn't care what ignorant naysayers called her, it stung anyway. She didn't understand why adults would attack her when she was trying to serve humanity. She was being the grown-up and they were being childish bullies.

When Jayla opened the door, she saw tears welling up in Ivy's eyes and immediately opened her arms wide to hug her friend. Through sobs and heaves, Jayla found out about the mean-spirited tweets from a particular immoral politician who made spearing Ivy his new sport. Jayla didn't have any words of wisdom to make the situation better. She knew Ivy just needed to cry. After a minute, Ivy calmed down and they nestled into the couch for a chat to unload the hurt. She knew Ivy didn't need advice, so she just listened.

Feeling better, Ivy took a deep breath and said, "Sorry I just burst through your door like that. Thanks for listening. How are you?"

"Oh, I'm fine. I'm writing a paper and it's boring. I needed a break from it," replied Jayla. "It's good timing."

"For Carlson's class?" asked Ivy.

Jayla nodded.

That's when Ivy asked Jayla the question that caused their biggest fight in eleven years of friendship. "Is that a new sweater?"

Jayla wanted to deny that she bought fast fashion on a whim because she knew it carried a high carbon footprint, but she didn't want to lie.

"Yeah," answered Jayla, hoping that short answer would suffice.

"Where did you get it?" questioned Ivy.

"Oh, it was a gift," Jayla lied.

"From who? Your birthday is in the summer and I saw everything you got for Christmas," replied Ivy.

Jayla knew she had trapped herself in a lie, so she confessed, "OK, Ivy, I bought it at the outlet mall. It's fast fashion. I know you're going to hate it."

Ivy stared at her in disbelief before asking, "Why did you buy it? You know it's not good for the planet."

Jayla, shook her head and replied, "I don't know, Ivy. I wanted a new sweater. I don't know what to buy. I know I should buy top-quality products that will last years so I can reduce my consumption, but it's so confusing. Cotton's no good, because of all the pesticides and intensive water use. Athleisure and synthetic clothes are petroleum products and 35 percent of the microplastic fibers that enter the ocean come from these synthetic textiles."[63]

Ivy actually didn't know if that statistic was correct but thought it sounded right and Jayla was pretty much never wrong.

Jayla continued, "Rayon cuts down forests and uses a ton of chemicals, so..."

"Just don't buy it! Or rent it from Rent the Runway!" interrupted Ivy, "Don't you know that cheap cashmere usually comes from goats raised in the Gobi Desert?[64] Livestock account for a ton of methane. And those goats rip out the vegetation from the roots that opens the land up to severe erosion!" snarled Ivy before she stormed out.

"What am I supposed to do? Go naked? I guess not everyone can be perfect like you!" hollered Jayla after her.

***

Ivy went home and sulked. Even her best friend was part of the problem, she ruminated.

Viola came into the living room to see her daughter splayed out on the couch with an angry look.

"What's the matter?" she asked.

Ivy told her mom about Jayla's sweater and about the tweets.

Her mom sat down next to her and said, "I'm so sorry about those nasty tweets. I know this won't help, but try to ignore those tweets. It sickens me that elected officials are allowed to behave like toddlers."

Ivy nodded.

"As for Jayla, let's step back from the situation for a minute. So, Jayla bought that sweater. Everyone consumes things every day. No one is without an environmental footprint. If we start pointing fingers at our best friends and family, we will never be able to work together as a society to solve the enormous problems we have. We can't get lost in nitpicking," said Viola gently.

Ivy knew her mom was right, and that she needed to apologize to Jayla for being self-righteous. It wasn't Jayla's fault that the clothing industry has such a frustrating lack of transparency with loads of greenwashing. And it was a cute sweater that looked amazing on her.

CHAPTER 29

Happiness Tips the Scales of Justice

"I have learned over the years that when one's mind is made up,
this diminishes fear; knowing what must be done does away with fear."
—Rosa Parks

As the Defenders of the Future watched society unravel, it was clear that additional long-term solutions were needed because greenhouse gas emissions were rising to unsustainable levels again. Their original plan to have the Ejecteds make emission reforms wasn't enough. The disinformation campaigns caused fear, unrest, stress, and anger—even between people sharing the same goals.

"Stop fighting and trying to be right!" hollered Seth as if people on Earth could hear him. "You're getting lost in the weeds and wasting valuable time! Perfection is the enemy of progress. Stop your fault finding! Don't you see how counter-productive it is?"

Aziza said, "We need a way to keep humanity focused—keep their eye on the prize of saving humanity. As Rosa Parks famously said, '...knowing what must be done does away with fear.' And what needs to be done is straight forward. We've got the policies and programs in place to bring down emissions and to support sustainable lifestyles. That's an amazing accomplishment! Now we need to turn down the panic."

Seth bellowed back, "Turn down the panic? Now is hardly the

time to turn down the panic, Aziza. The situation is black and white. The house is on fire! They need to get out NOW and call 911 from the neighbor's! They need to go full speed ahead!"

"True enough," replied Aziza calmly, "but panic only causes fear and stress hormones that will paralyze people and continue this in-fighting we are witnessing."

Seth scrunched his eyes tightly to process Aziza's point and then nodded, "I guess you're right."

Aziza continued, "At this point, we need to do away with the negatives and focus on getting people to be on the same team. Maybe we can increase team participation by reminding people how lovely and rewarding living a simpler lifestyle is. How about we teach people to tap into their natural 'happiness' brain chemicals that are fostered by living a voluntarily simple lifestyle? Scaring people into action has never worked long term."

***

Salomon found Keith sitting on his and Viola's deck enjoying the warmth of the spring sunshine on his face. He was just thinking about that it had been nearly a year since he was ejected when Salomon appeared unexpectedly in front of him.

After a friendly greeting, Salomon explained why he was there, "The first simple step to make the transition to voluntary simplicity easier for people is to help them tap into their 'happiness' brain chemicals: dopamine, oxytocin, serotonin, and endorphins that are a natural fit with living a balanced and healthy voluntary simple lifestyle."

Intrigued, Keith said, "Oh?"

Salomon continued, "Yes, for example, dopamine, often called the 'the reward chemical,' can be obtained through completing tasks, celebrating small wins, self-care activities, volunteering, loving thoughts, and eating wonderful food. That type of stuff. All of these things are easier to do when living a slower-paced, simpler lifestyle, and therefore, go a long way to support dopamine levels and encourage people to stick with the lifestyle.

"Makes sense," agreed Keith.

Salomon continued, "Oxytocin is 'the love hormone' that is typically achieved through physical contact with other living beings."

"Yes, like holding a baby," said Keith reminiscing rocking Ivy. "So, connecting with friends, family, and the community helps boost those levels, right?" asked Keith.

"Exactly. And serotonin—kind of a 'mood stabilizer'—is attained through sunshine, connection with nature, exercise, and meditation. Again, healthy serotonin levels go hand-in-hand with the hashtag Victory Life," said Salomon.

Hearing his grandpa, who looked like a teenager, say "hashtag" made Keith laugh.

"And, I see you're increasing your endorphins by laughing at me," Salomon said as he smiled.

"I'd like to say I'm laughing with you, not at you," said Keith. "I thought endorphins were the natural pain killers—the runner's high."

"Indeed," agreed Salomon, "All of these 'happiness' brain chemicals can be boosted many ways. Exercise helps with serotonin and endorphin levels. We really need to keep people focused on the big picture and not sweating the small stuff. Otherwise, we're going to see a whole lot of fighting over insignificant details without moving forward in reducing our emissions."

***

Thankfully, focusing on the positives—like kindness, gratitude, connecting with nature, laughter, helping the future, and good food grown and prepared by the community—helped steer society back to uniting around the urgent world situation. Since the world still remembered those harmonious six weeks after the Ejected returned to Earth, it was easier to get back to that place. There was a general consensus that it didn't make sense to argue about trivial details when looming catastrophes threatened human species' survival. Over and over, the mantra was to focus on what needed to be accomplished and what united people, rather than what divided them.

A new social contract was built around universal care, meaning getting every individual's basic needs met. It became socially unacceptable to put ones' needs above their communities' needs. Gentleness and harmony were cherished while aggression, violence, self-centeredness, and material self-interest were discouraged. The majority of humanity understood that in order to overcome the climate crisis, people had to put their differences aside and focus on the common good. The threats that faced the planet could only be met if there was lockstep action. They had ten years to sort this all out. They didn't have time for pettiness. But in order to have unity, injustices everywhere needed to be addressed and resolved quickly.

Workplace trainings and schools taught empathy and compassion. Emotional intelligence was regarded as being just as important, if not more important, than standard core subjects like reading and math. People worked diligently to reach understanding with others and realized that since everyone starts from their own viewpoint, they likely perceive themselves as being correct. People had to renew their commitments daily—sometimes even hourly—to work to understand others' points of view. It was challenging, but necessary.

This new decarbonized society also valued and embraced differences. There was an effort to find a valuable place for everyone, since everyone had something special to share. With people feeling valued, they were inclined to pay kindness and generosity forward. People were taught to find and use their strengths to let their inner lights shine for the good of the world. Every talent was seen as having equal significance because it was known that each step would lead to the next step and neither the first step nor the last are of greater significance. All steps, large and small, are needed to reduce emissions.

Young children were taught that kindness started with them. They couldn't wait for others to be kind first. They were taught that there may be scarcity of many natural resources, but there is an abundance of love; whatever a being puts out into the universe comes back to them—positive or negative.

✱✱✱

The second part of the plan included developing impartial scales of justice that would keep people from worrying about their own CO_2e footprints and feeling the need to judge others' footprints. The goal of this scale was to allow people to relax and focus on themselves. These scales were highly experimental and the calculations were immensely complicated. The scales were calibrated for each individual and "fair" wasn't necessarily equal. People with different opportunities, dietary needs, as well as physical and mental abilities, weren't evaluated with the same point system. Every minute detail was personalized and accounted for. But the most incredible feature of these scales was their ability to measure a person's intentions and commitments!

Everyone was encouraged to weigh in periodically to see if lifestyle adjustments were needed to regulate their CO_2e footprints. The scales were intentionally located in remote areas surrounded by nature, so people had to get a little exercise to get to the scale. The sunshine, exercise, connection with nature, and feeling of accomplishment by completing the hike boosted brain chemicals and made the weigh in fun.

At the end of the weigh-in, participants were rewarded with a long list of the positive things they were doing well to keep those dopamine levels high as well as honest feedback on an area or two that were growth opportunities for them.

The system certainly wasn't perfect, but it was overall very well-received and improved over time. Best of all, it kept people from being hypercritical of others and it ensured that no one used more than their share.

If the scale gave a failing "weight," meaning a person's emission levels were too high, that person would need to make adjustments to their life. Many people teetered on the edge of going over their emissions limit, so grace was granted when people went over for a time. The most important factor was that people made an effort.

When corrective measures didn't work, individuals were further counselled about the Earth's limitations and reminded that the planet might not be able to continue supporting them. If after repeated intervention attempts, people continued to burden society with excessive consumption, their fate was up to the scales. Since the scales used raw data, it wasn't an act of malice, but rather an act of necessity to keep the people on Earth healthy. And, although always regrettable, those self-centered people who just wouldn't play for team humanity would have to be...

ejected.

Notes

1   Jonathan Watts, "Climate change science pioneer Wallace Smith Broecker dies," *The Guardian*, February 19, 2019, https://www.theguardian.com/science/2019/feb/19/climate-change-science-pioneer-wallace-smith-broecker-dies

2   Intergovernmental Panel on Climate Change, et al., "The Effects of Climate Change," *NASA Global Climate Change*, https://climate.nasa.gov/effects/

3   Intergovernmental Panel on Climate Change, et al., "The Effects of Climate Change."

4   Georgina Gustin, "25 Fossil Fuel Producers Responsible for Half Global Emissions in Past 3 Decades," *Inside Climate News*, July 9, 2017, https://insideclimatenews.org/news/10072017/fossil-fuel-companies-responsible-global-emissions-cdp-report

5   Gustin, "25 Fossil Fuel Producers Responsible for Half Global Emissions in Past 3 Decades."

6   Kathleen Ebbitt, "5 facts on climate refugees-and why you should care," *Global Citizen*, June 8, 2015, https://www.globalcitizen.org/en/content/5-facts-on-climate-refugees-and-why-you-should-car/

7   Tedros Adhanom Ghebreyesus, "Climate Change is Already Killing Us," *Foreign Affairs*, September 23, 2019, https://www.foreignaffairs.com/articles/2019-09-23/climate-change-already-killing-us

8   Joel Makower, "COVID-19 and climate change: A healthy dose of reality," *GreenBiz*, March 16, 2020, https://www.greenbiz.com/article/covid-19-and-climate-change-healthy-dose-reality

9   Makower, "COVID-19 and climate change: A healthy dose of reality."

10   Worldometer, May 12, 2020, https://www.worldometers.info/coronavirus/

11   "Climate Change Impacts by Region," *U.S. Environmental Protection Agency*, January 19, 2017, https://19january2017snapshot.epa.gov/climate-impacts/climate-change-impacts-region_.html

12   "Climate Change Impacts by Region," *U.S. Environmental Protection Agency*.

13   "Climate Change Impacts by Region," *U.S. Environmental Protection Agency*.

14   "Climate Change Impacts by Region," *U.S. Environmental Protection Agency*.

15   "Climate Change Impacts by Region," *U.S. Environmental Protection Agency*.

16   "The Effects of Climate Change," *NASA*, climate.nasa.gove/effects/

17   En-ROADS, *Climate Interactive and MIT Management Sustainability Initiative*, https://en-roads.climateinteractive.org/scenario.html?p1=120&p7=100&p10=6&p16=-0.07&p23=30&p35=2&p39=250&p47=5&p50=5&p53=5&p55=5&p67=4&v=2.7.29&units=us

18   "The Globe Is Already Above 1 °C, on Its Way to 1.5 °C," *Climate Central, October 9, 2018* https://www.climatecentral.org/gallery/graphics/the-globe-is-already-above-1c

19   "Limiting Global Warming to 1.5°C Will Require Deep Emissions Cuts," *Climate Central,* October 9, 2018, https://www.climatecentral.org/gallery/graphics/limiting-global-warming-require-deep-emissions-cuts

20   "Each Country's Share of CO_2 Emissions," *Union of Concerned Scientists*, May 11, 2020 https://www.ucsusa.org/resources/each-countrys-share-co2-emissions

21   Hannah Richie and Max Roser, "CO_2 and Greenhouse Gas Emissions," *Our World Data,* December 2019, https://ourworldindata.org/co2-and-other-greenhouse-gas-emissions#cumulative-co2-emissions

22   *Worldometer,* May 12, 2020, https://www.worldometers.info/

world-population/us-population/

23   Tejvan Pettinger, "Top CO_2 polluters and highest per capita," *Economics Help*, October 25, 2019, https://www.economicshelp. org/blog/10296/economics/top-co2-polluters-highest-per-capita/

24   "Stopping Climate Change: A Practical Plan 3 Tons Carbon Dioxide Per Person Per Year," *EcoCivilization*, https://www. ecocivilization.info/three-tons-carbon-dioxide-per-person-per-year.html

25   "Cooler Smarter: Geek Out on the Data!" *Union of Concerned Scientists*, March 29, 2012, https://www.ucsusa.org/resources/ cooler-smarter-geek-out-data#.W-4zk-hKjD5

26   Vann R. Newkirk II, "Trump's EPA Concludes Environmental Racism Is Real, A new report from the Environmental Protection Agency finds that people of color are much more likely to live near polluters and breathe polluted air—even as the agency seeks to roll back regulations on pollution," *The Atlantic*, February 28, 2018, https://www.theatlantic.com/ politics/archive/2018/02/the-trump-administration-finds-that-environmental-racism-is-real/554315/

27   "Fossil fuels continue to account for the largest share of U.S. energy," *U.S. Energy Information Administration*, September 18, 2019, https://www.eia.gov/todayinenergy/detail.php?id=41353

28   En-ROADS, *Climate Interactive and MIT Management Sustainability Initiative*, https://en-roads.climateinteractive.org/ scenario.html?v=2.7.19

29   "Rondo Neighborhood & I-94," *Minnesota Historical Society Library*, https://libguides.mnhs.org/rondo

30   Greta Kaul, "With covenants, racism was written into Minneapolis housing. The scars are still visible," *MinnPost*, February 22, 2019, https://www.minnpost.com/metro/2019/02/ with-covenants-racism-was-written-into-minneapolis-housing-the-scars-are-still-visible/

31   Kaul, "With covenants, racism was written into Minneapolis housing. The scars are still visible,"

32   Ann Bailey, "Breaking Down the Typical Utility Bill," *Energy Star*, https://www.energystar.gov/products/ask-the-expert/

breaking-down-the-typical-utility-bill

33 "Environmental Impacts of Natural Gas," *Union of Concerned Scientists*, June 19, 2014, https://ucsusa.org/resources/environmental-impacts-natural-gas

34 "Freshwater Use by U.S Power Plants: Electricity's Thirst for a Precious Resource," *Union of Concerned Scientists*, November 16, 2011 https://www.ucsusa.org/resources/freshwater-use-us-power-plants

35 "Freshwater Use by U.S Power Plants: Electricity's Thirst for a Precious Resource," *Union of Concerned Scientists*.

36 Mike Berners-Lee, "How Bad Are Bananas?: The Carbon Footprint of Everything," April 1, 2011, (London: Greystone Books, 2011), 73

37 Joe Wachunas, "Hang Drying Revolution," Green Living, https://www.greenlivingpdx.com/hang-drying-revolution/?fbclid=IwAR2WVJAx7ORg_Ofhg1hD34IMdz9QmPDXbL0O4eYud0Ucn5wD3MDN0BYN7G8

38 Wachunas, "Hang Drying Revolution."

39 Wachunas, "Hang Drying Revolution."

40 Wachunas, "Hang Drying Revolution."

41 Wachunas, "Hang Drying Revolution."

42 Gabe Brown, "Regeneration of Our Lands: A Producer's Perspective," *TEDxGrandForks*, March 29, 2016, https://www.youtube.com/watch?v=QfTZ0rnowcc

43 Global Emissions by Economic Sector, *U.S. Environmental Protection Agency*, January 19, 2017, https://www.epa.gov/ghgemissions/global-greenhouse-gas-emissions-data

44 Prajakta Dhapte, "These Are The Worst Smells in The World, According to Science," August 5, 2018, *Science Alert*, https://www.sciencealert.com/what-are-the-worst-smells-in-the-world-according-to-science

45 Paul Hawkin, "Reduced Food Waste," April 18, 2018, *Drawdown*, https://drawdown.org/solutions/reduced-food-waste

46 Hawkin, "Reduced Food Waste," https://drawdown.org/solutions/reduced-food-waste

47 Maria LaMagna, "Americans throw out about $165 billion worth of food every year," August 8, 2017, *Market Watch*, https://www.marketwatch.com/story/why-supermarkets-want-to-sell-you-ugly-fruits-and-vegetables-2016-08-06

48 Hawkin, "Biogas for Cooking," https://drawdown.org/solutions/biogas-for-cooking

49 Hawkin, "Biogas for Cooking."

50 Berners-Lee, "How Bad Are Bananas?: The Carbon Footprint of Everything," 125.

51 Beth Daley, "Bike-friendly cities should be designed for everyone, not just for wealthy white cyclists," *The Conversation*, August 23, 2019, https://theconversation.com/bike-friendly-cities-should-be-designed-for-everyone-not-just-for-wealthy-white-cyclists-109485

52 Juli Berwal, "One overlooked way to fight climate change? Dispose of old CFCs." *National Geographic*, April 29, 2019, https://www.nationalgeographic.com/environment/2019/04/disposing-old-cfcs-refrigerants-reduces-climate-change-greenhouse-gases-cheaply/

53 Berwal, "One overlooked way to fight climate change? Dispose of old CFCs."

54 Berwal, "One overlooked way to fight climate change? Dispose of old CFCs."

55 Dawn Gifford, "How to Stop Population Growth—Humanely," *Small Footprint Family*, https://www.smallfootprintfamily.com/how-to-stop-population-growth#ixzz6CeEO9nTb

56 Berners-Lee, "How Bad Are Bananas?: The Carbon Footprint of Everything." 199.

57 Thomas Friedman, "The First Law of Petropolitics," October 16, 2009, *Foreign Policy*, https://foreignpolicy.com/2009/10/16/the-first-law-of-petropolitics/

58 Doug Moss and Roddy Scheer, "Junk mail impacts carbon levels," May 30, 2015, *Poughkeepsie Journal*, https://www.poughkeepsiejournal.com/story/life/2015/05/30/junk-mail-impacts-carbon-levels/28076557/

59 "The Carbon Footprint of the Internet," April 13, 2015, *Custom*

Made, https://www.custommade.com/blog/carbon-footprint-of-internet/

60   "The Carbon Footprint of the Internet," *Custom Made.*

61   "The Carbon Footprint of the Internet," *Custom Made.*

62   Michael Bloch, "Phantom Electricity Loads=Higher Power Bills and Carbon Emissions, August 2, 2012, *Green Living Tips,* https://www.greenlivingtips.com/articles/standby-power-electricity-consumption.html

63   Tatiana Schlossberg, "Inconspicuous Consumption: The Environmental Impact You Don't Know You Have," (New York: Grand Central Publishing, 2019): 263

64   Schlossberg, "Inconspicuous consumption,": 161-165

Educational Resources

Climate Interactive

climateinteractive.org

> Climate Interactive creates accessible, scientifically rigorous tools that help people see connections, play out scenarios, and see what works to address the biggest challenges we face.

Climate Generation—A Will Steger Legacy

climategen.org

> Empowers individuals and their communities to engage in solutions to climate change. Curriculum, training for teachers, opportunities for students, climate school board resolutions and more.

Project Drawdown

drawdown.org

> Helping the world reach "Drawdown"— the point in the future when levels of greenhouse gases in the atmosphere stop climbing and start to steadily decline, thereby stopping catastrophic climate change — as quickly, safely, and equitably as possible.

We All Need Food and Water

weallneedfoodandwater.org

> Educates about challenges facing our food and water systems through a variety of programming to inspire action.

Lightning Source UK Ltd.
Milton Keynes UK
UKHW020630031020
370957UK00006B/234